CW00795271

TALES OF ARTHUR

Adventure Stories from the Arthurian Legend

John Matthews & Bob Stewart

J

JAVELIN BOOKS

LONDON . NEW YORK . SYDNEY

This edition first published in the UK 1988 by Javelin Books, an imprint of
Cassell plc (original)
Artillery House, Artillery Row, London SW1P 1RT

Stories first published in *Warriors of Arthur* in the UK 1987 by Blandford Press Ltd.

Copyright © 1987 and 1988 John Matthews and Robert John Stewart

Distributed in the United States by
Sterling Publishing Co., Inc.,
2 Park Avenue, New York, NY 10016

Distributed in Australia by
Capricorn Link (Australia) Pty Ltd,
PO Box 665, Lane Cove, NSW 2066

British Library Cataloguing in Publication Data

Matthews, John, *1948–*
Tales of Arthur : adventure stories from
the Arthurian legend.
I. Title   II. Stewart, Bob
823'.914[F]

ISBN 0–7137–2059–X

All rights reserved. No part of this book may
be reproduced or transmitted in any form or by
any means, electronic or mechanical, including
photocopying, recording or any information storage
and retrieval system, without permission in writing from the publisher.

This book is sold subject to the conditions that it shall not, by way of
trade or otherwise, be lent, re-sold, hired out or otherwise circulated
without the publisher's prior consent in any form of binding or cover
other than that in which it is published and without a similar condition
including this condition being imposed on the subsequent purchaser.

Typset by Inforum Ltd, Portsmouth

Made and printed in Great Britain by
The Guernsey Press Co. Ltd., Guernsey, Channel Islands.

Contents

Introduction

THERE ARE SIX stories in this book, three by each author, and each with a short introduction. We make no excuses for these retellings as they are directly within the mainstream of Arthurian legend and history. Nevertheless, before the tales were written some firm rules of conduct were established, and these are worth outlining in advance.

Firstly there is no obscure stylism, none of the quirky pseudo-medieval linguistics that editors call 'Arthur-speak'; the language is intentionally direct and simple. Secondly there is no Celtic twilight glimmering around the vocabulary; we have not employed obscure Welsh terms, for example, that might mean little to the modern reader. Any such terms have been given modern English equivalents. This is the root of the matter, for any story is, or should be, utterly contemporary to the people within it.

We have aimed to re-tell a selection of classic Arthurian legends without any derivative medieval or later accumulation; they are set in a period between the fourth and sixth centuries, and the matters of which they speak are those which concerned the people of that period.

To come to some understanding of Arthur and his warriors and people we must always remember that they revived a genuine culture of heroic imaginative dimensions; the magical elements were not merely grafted onto obscure semi-history by later writers, but are inherent in the British Celtic inspiration and traditions. Arthur was perhaps the first consciously British (Celtic) king after the collapse of Roman influence . . . it is this revival of native culture, so strong in the fifth and sixth centuries, that caused numerous legends and traditions to become magnetically drawn to the figures of the king and his warriors and their consorts. Stories would have been central to the daily life of the Arthurian court; both stories and songs preserved the original legends well into the medieval period, and certain themes have persisted in folk traditions even into the nineteenth and twentieth centuries.

It would not be too excessive to say that a culture such as that of sixth-century Britain was held together by its songs, tales, and communal store of education and imagination. In times of stress and invasion, such elements of the shared consciousness come even more strongly to the forefront of family, group, tribe or national activity. We know that extensive Welsh and Scottish traditions were preserved well into the twelfth century, and for many years beyond, as we have written records such as the *Mabinogion* or the ubiquitous *History of the British Kings*. Apart from the resurgence of national identity in a historical context which supports a culture held together in time of stress, we have a direct modern parallel in the famous behaviour of the British during the Blitz. Personal concerns were temporarily laid aside, and without an enduring store of tradition people still created unity through popular songs and entertainments. This is a typical example of how communal tradition supports people in difficult circumstances; it remains to be seen in the future whether or not widespread television has finally destroyed this communality that

8

appeared in such an attenuated form during the Second World War.

In the re-tellings of Arthurian legends, we selected six themes which have quite widespread variants, both primitive and literary. They are told in such a way that both reader and teller are supposed to be part of a living culture . . . there is no suggestion of alienation or separation or academic speciality. The stories are to be enjoyed, not dissected. In some cases there are stories within stories, and they are told by people already in a historical Arthurian setting; examples of this are dealt with in our brief introductions which give basic historical connectives where necessary. As one might expect, two major themes emerged when we began to work on the tales: battle or warfare on both individual and national scales; and the magical or otherworldly elements which are fundamental both to Celtic culture in general and to Arthurian lore in particular.

We have not neglected the essential aspect of feminine power and awareness; later medieval legends moved towards the theme of courtly love, but this is firmly rooted in a more ancient source, where women are equally as powerful as men . . . and in some cases superior. There is little doubt when we examine Celtic tradition that while action and heroism come from men, wisdom, education and initiation are the gift of women. In later literature, this potent feminine influence, once defined as the power of ancient goddesses, is heavily corrupted sometimes to the extent that Arthurian heroines are merely wilting stereotypes being alternatively courted, seduced and abused by musclebound mail-clad knights. The same corruption has crept into the tales regarding Merlin, who in his earliest records is guided and advised by a feminine power, but by the Victorian era is shown as being seduced and enervated by a ludicrous vamp. No such stereotypes were allowed when our tales were planned and we trust that they have not sneaked their way into the final tellings.

As has been repeatedly proven by the success of historical novels, the imagination is greatly fired by details of the past brought to life from a factual foundation. On a historical level Arthur tried to revitalise and unify a British culture, and out of this obscure historical period emerge legends and mythical patterns of human unity, even of spiritual vision, which are unquestionably holistic. The fights against savagery, the order of honourable warriors, the Round Table, the essential significance of feminine power, the ultimate quest for truth in the form of the Grail . . . all attempt to fuse historical and imaginative elements together and pass them on to future generations.

Our aim has been less exalted, of course, and if we have given the reader some insight into the true nature of the roots of Arthurian history and tradition, we are temporarily content. Why temporarily? Because, like the famous *Prophecies of Merlin* which are given fresh meaning as each generation considers them in retrospect, Arthurian studies and developments will always change and expand. Hence our statement at the opening of this section, in which we claim that our re-tellings are directly within the mainstream of Arthurian legend and history . . . for it is a source, a cauldron of inspiration, for the historian, archaeologist, sociologist, psychologist, and most important of all for those who tell and those who read and listen to stories.

Lugh Strong-Arm & The Three Queens

I N THE MEDIEVAL romances the figure of Sir Lancelot of the Lake is in the forefront of Arthur's knights. He displaced earlier heroes, such as Gawain and Kei, and became the premier Knight of the Round Table, unbeaten in each single-combat or tournament until the coming of his strange and saintly son Galahad, the Grail winner.

Many scholars have followed the belief that Lancelot was an invention of the fertile brain of Chrétien de Troyes. However, an alternative theory suggests that behind the tremendous figure of the medieval knight stands a succession of older, Celtic heroes, of the kind more appropriate to the historical Arthurian period.

Amongst the most prominent of these are Lugh Loinn-bheimionach and Llwch Llemineawg, originally the same character but subsequently split into Irish and Welsh aspects. Both were noted for their strength, fiery disposition and the possession of magical weapons – a spear which roared for blood in the case of the Irish Lugh, and a flaming sword in that of the Welsh Llwch.

In the story which follows is told one of the most famous episodes from the life of Lancelot – his encounter with three magical women of Arthurian Britain. However, in this version, which should be seen as told by one of the wandering story-tellers likely to have been found at Arthur's court, it is Lancelot's earlier self who is the protagonist.

The three queens themselves, in the medieval version Morgan le Fay, Morgana and the unnamed Queen of Norgalles, can be seen as representing ancient Celtic matriarchal themes, or at a deeper, still more ancient level, as debased aspects of the Triple Goddess, worshipped throughout the Western world during the Bronze Age and after.

The description of the otherworldly realm in which Lugh/Lancelot is imprisoned is consistent with details to be found in numerous Celtic stories – as is the belief that while the denizens of Faery may capture the body of a human being, they have no power over his or her soul, and therefore cannot compel either to act against their will.

Time is either without meaning or of a different order in Faery. When the Irish hero Bran son of Febal visited the Land of Women (a place not unlike that in which Lugh is here confined), though he remained there for what seemed to him only a few months, when he returned to the real world he found all whom he had known were long dead. He himself had become legendary.

The final paragraph of the story refers to another episode from the life of Lancelot – how a maiden from the land of Astolat fell in love with him and how, when her passion was unrequited, she died and her body was ferried downriver to the walls of Camelot, together with a letter which told her story. In Malory this has become part of the world of chivalry and courtly love; Tennyson retold it in the nineteenth century in his poem *The Lady of Shalott*; the version offered here is merely a speculation as to the origin of the story.

The story I have to tell is of Lugh of the Strong-Arm in the days before he became one of Arthur's men and of that company the greatest champion and most feared warrior of all. Even then he had the kind of face that drew the attentions of women and led him into adventures from which only the swiftness of his sword-arm – and sometimes of his feet – drew him whole.

On this occasion of which I speak the hero had gone hunting alone, and such was his success that by noon of the day he had enough meat to feed even the Cauldron of Dwrnach the Giant for more nights than one. Now in the heat of the day there came upon him a great desire for sleep, for he had hunted well and come far from his home-run. And so, having stacked his hunting spears carefully against the bole of a great tree, Lugh cast himself down in its shade and fell into a light sleep – though always his hand lay near to his sword, and he twitched in his sleep like a hound before the fire.

While he lay thus, there was a movement in the forest, and there came into view as strange a procession as any you might see in that time and place. First there came a dwarf carrying a great spear on which was set a freshly severed head – the mouth still gaped in its death shout and blood darkened the shaft of the spear. Behind this came four ill-shaped creatures, dressed in skins, who seemed as though they had once been tall men, but who now shambled and dragged themselves along like broken beasts. Above them they supported a canopy of rich cloth, finer than anything seen in those parts, and beneath its shade, sitting upon three white ponies, with saddle-cloths of softest sheepskin, were three women of such beauty you would have thought they came of the Underland itself. They were dressed in such richness as might have shamed the court of Melwas, King of the Summer Country, himself.

13

Now when these three saw where Lugh of the Strong-Arm lay beneath the tree, they stopped, and seeing how his hand lay close to his broad-hafted sword and how his spears stood close at hand, one of them raised her hand and drew upon the air a sign that caused the hero at once to fall into a sleep from which none could have wakened him, save she who cast it upon him.

Then the three got down from their mounts and came nearer, and when they looked upon the sleeping youth and remarked upon his beauty and the play of his muscles beneath his breathing skin, they at once fell to arguing. For, said she who had laid the sleep-without-dreams upon him, this was surely the most beautiful creature they had seen this long while and he must surely be intended for her. And she had hair the colour of a raven's wing and secret eyes, and her mouth was the colour of rowan berries and her form was fair, and her name was Morgana, though in those days she was not so well known in the Lowlands as now she is

And her sisters, who were called Morgause and Argante, were equally fair, and the first had hair like a sunset and the second like a bright golden net; and they were all three touched with the gleam of twilight and the radiance of inner earth. And when they looked upon Lugh where he lay they all three cast lustful thought towards him, and began to dispute with each other – for it seemed to them that all might have sport with this young hero; but as to who should have him first they could not agree. And so at last Morgana, who was the eldest, said: 'Let us take him to a safer place than this and, when he wakes, let him decide which of us three he shall have first.' And by their arts – for they were indeed partly of Elvish stock and well-versed in the magic arts – they went from that place to another, deeper in the wood-wards of the forest, taking the sleeping hero with them, so that when he woke at last, stretching and turning like one who has slept overlong, he found that he was in a place where branches of hawthorn met over him, and that a barrier of thorns was on every side, so that he was as much a prisoner as if he had been held in a room of stone. Further, he saw that his weapons had all been taken from him while he slept, but that food – fair, small cakes and a bowl of good beer – had been left by his side. And though he knew the prohibition against eating the food of Faery, yet he was young enough to put the needs of the belly before thought of danger; so he ate and drank his fill and then sat down upon the ground and drew his knees up to his chin and waited for what would occur . . .

And what did occur was this: there came a high, clear, far-off seeming voice that said words which Lugh could neither hear nor understand – except that it made the hairs on his neck stand up, while a shiver ran through him like one who sees his own grave. Then there came into his prison – though how he could not see, since there seemed no entrance or exit – three beautiful women (for such at least he supposed them to be) who stood close together as though they were each part of a whole, and looked at him. Then Morgana – though he did not know it was she – said, 'You are called Lugh of the Strong-Arm, and you will be the greatest warrior ever to walk in the halls of the Lord Arthur.' Now this meant nothing to Lugh since the name of Arthur was little known at that time; but he stood up slowly and looked at the three women in the eyes as unflinchingly as he could; though he could not help a small gleed of fear that needed little to fan it into flame. 'As to that,' he said, 'you seem to know well enough who I am; but I would as soon know who it is that has brought me here.'

'We are the Queens of the North and of the South and of the East,' said Morgause, 'and we have brought you here

15

that you might choose which of us you will have for your lover.'

'As to that,' Lugh replied, 'if I truly have a choice, then I might refuse you all.'

The three queens drew even closer together and it seemed for a moment that Lugh saw before him a great serpent whose scales shone green in the strange light of that place, and that it hissed and spat at him. Then Argante, she of the hair like a spun-gold net, spoke up for the first time: 'Listen well, warrior,' she said, 'it would be easy for us to compel you to our need, but it is our will that you choose one of us to lie with. Therefore we shall leave you to think upon this, since we understand that it is no easy thing for any mortal to choose from three such as we. But we shall return shortly and you must choose by then.' And before Lugh might protest further he found that he was alone, though the manner of the three women's exit he still could not guess. Then he fell to thinking, and he seemed to remember the four broken creatures who had carried the canopy above the three, and in his mind he understood that such would be his own fate if he took any one of the queens to his bed – for though he was young and lusty enough to feel desire for all three, yet he knew also that to love such as they brought only pain and fretful longings, and in that place of thorns and dim, unfocused light, he felt a great longing to feel the air of the outside world upon his face, and to see the sun again. And his spirit felt heavy and chill, and he chafed to hold a sword in his hand with which to cut his way out of that place. . . .

Then he heard a voice which spoke to him from beyond the imprisoning hedge, and which asked him how he fared. 'Not well,' he answered, 'nor is it likely to get better.' At that there was an audible sigh and a small hole appeared in the spiked thickness of the hedge, and through the hole came a slim white arm and hand, offering a dish of food and a vessel of beer. Lugh took these and said, 'Who is it that asks after my well being?'

'A prisoner, like yourself.'

'And have you a name, fellow-prisoner?'

'I had . . . once, but one soon forgets.'

'Then do you know where this place is?'

'O yes, this place is nowhere and everywhere and some-where.'

'That is no answer.'

But the arm and hand withdrew and at once the hole closed up, leaving Lugh alone once more. He ate and drank and walked around the confines of the hedge and tried to see what lay beyond it, but there was only uniform greyness where there were chinks in the living wall of his prison; and there was only silence save for the sound of his own breathing. . . .

In that place time had no dimension, so that Lugh had no way of telling how long he remained there. Twice more the three queens came to visit him, and each time he refused them. Once, they showed him pictures in his mind of the methods they would use to persuade him; and once they showed him what pleasures he might enjoy if he gave in to their desires; but in spite of this they did nothing to compel him, and in his heart Lugh began to believe that they could not, that he must give willingly what they sought.

And when next the hole appeared in the hedge, and the owner of the slim white arm came with food and drink for him, he asked if this was true.

'It is true that they cannot take what you do not give; but in time you will be glad enough to do what they desire.'

'Is that why you do their bidding?'

'Yes.'

'But why do you not try to escape?'

'Why do *you* not try?'

'Because I am a prisoner behind this hedge of thorns.'

At this there was silence for a time, but at length the voice spoke again. 'There is no hedge; our bonds are of another kind.'

'But if there is no hedge, then how is it that I can see and feel it; and how is it that all I can see of yourself is an arm and a hand?' But all the voice would say was that there was no hedge.

But in a while he heard the voice again, and this time it said, 'The Three have been talking together and they have decided that if you do not choose one of them today they will kill you.'

'What can I do?' Lugh asked.

'Do you wish to escape?'

'There is nothing I would liefer do.'

'Then take my hand and believe that what I say is true,' and once again the slim white arm and hand appeared through the hedge and Lugh took it. But still he hesitated. 'Hurry!' came the voice, 'Why do you hesitate? The Three are coming.' At which Lugh closed his eyes and in desperation pressed himself upon the hedge of thorns. But where he had thought to feel their harsh pricking he felt nothing but air, and when he opened his eyes, he found that he stood upon a green mound and that his hand was clasping that of a slender girl whose black hair and red mouth and bright eyes reminded him of a blackbird. She pulled hard at his hand and urged him to hurry. 'For the Three are near, and once they discover that you have escaped they will surely pursue us to the very edge of the world.'

Lugh looked behind him and saw only a featureless greyness on every side, and nowhere that might be called an end to the sky or the land, if such indeed there were. 'How may we escape?' he said.

'There are twelve gates to this place,' said the girl, 'and if you will but trust me I shall lead you through them all.'

And Lugh looked at her and knew that this was no trick, and when she offered him her hand again he took it in his own without hesitation and followed where she led.

And that was the strangest journey that Lugh Strong-Arm ever took, even in time to come when he undertook many deeds in the name of Arthur, but he never forgot it, though if you were to ask him the how and the where of it he could not tell you. Only that there was much that seemed real and much unreal. Faces and voices and hands challenged them, but always the girl had answers for them where he would have had none, so that they came past each one until at last they stood in what seemed the entrance to a wood and there were two great trees on either side of it like sentinels and here his guide stopped.

'This is the last gate of all,' she said, 'and through it I may not pass. But to you I will teach the way so that you may depart.'

'But surely if I may pass then so may you?' But the girl shook her head. 'I have been here too long. If I were to step beyond that gate I should at once crumble to dust,' and Lugh remembered a story he had heard of a warrior who had returned after what seemed only a few days in the Land of Dreams and it was in truth a hundred years that had passed. 'Then how may I thank you?' he asked.

'I ask only that you remember me,' said the girl. 'Who knows, perhaps I may find a way to escape. If not, I shall be here when *you* are dust.'

And then she taught Lugh the secret words by which he might pass by the guardians of that last gate, and when he had spoken them he found himself in a part of the wood that he knew. But of the entrance to that strange world in which he had been a prisoner he could see nothing.

And it is told that Lugh Strong-Arm was changed from that time forth, and began to follow the course which brought him to the place of Arthur's greatest hero. But it is said also that of that time came the sealing of his fate, for when the three queens found that their prize was gone, they laid this *geas* upon him: that he should find love only with one woman, and that one, another's. But the gift of forgetting they withheld, so that even when Lugh became the lover of Guenhwyfar the Queen, he might not forget she who had rescued him from prison. And this was the reason (though none knew it then), that when, long after, a barge drifted down to Camulodunum the Great, bearing within it the body of a fair young girl with dark hair and white arms crossed upon her breast, that Lugh wept long and bitterly for what had been stolen from him when he scarcely knew what he had lost.

The Blundering Hero

THE QUEST FOR the Grail is central to Arthurian literature, but much of the Grail material was added slowly, accumulating mainly in the Middle Ages, several hundred years after the historical Arthur. There is, however, one theme (found in the *Mabinogion* in the long complex tale of *Peredur*) which seems to be the foundation of the highly sophisticated Grail legends. That theme is retold here as the tale of the Blundering Hero, and his name has been kept as Peredur even though he might have had many names during his heroic career in generations of retelling.

The theme behind the Grail legends is very ancient indeed, involving a series of mythical or religious motifs which were central to Celtic culture, in particular that of the cult of the sacred head. In early Celtic sites archaeologists have found sanctuaries for preserved human heads, plus carvings of heads of later date. We also know from classical sources that the early Celts were head-hunters who preserved their trophies in cedar oil or by some similar means. This savage ritual behaviour evolved into a cult and pattern of magical-religious thought which is still mysterious to us today; it also laid the foundations for one of the most profoundly sophisticated spiritual legends of the world, that of the Quest for the Holy Grail. Not until the twelfth or thirteenth century did the fusion of esoteric Christian and pagan Celtic traditions flower as the Grail legends.

How might such mystical or magical lore have been presented and preserved in the sixth century, and how might it have related to the historical Arthur? We can be sure that tales and customs involving sacred heads or skulls were active at that time, and that they were connected to themes of the health of the land, or to the sanctity of certain wells and springs. Furthermore, we may reasonably assume that some of these ancient practices were active within the early Christian Church, as so much effort was made on the part of the political Roman Church to suppress heresy in Britain and Gaul from the fourth century onwards.

Our tale, therefore, is set initially in a Celtic church sanctuary or chapel, in which an acolyte is being taught by a rather strange saint. It is this elder, Father Melchior, who actually tells the tale of Peredur to his anonymous pupil.

Some of the matters touched upon in his retelling would have been crucial to sixth-century Britain, as they involve the relationship between pagan traditions and Christianity, and the dramatic issue of the Roman Church versus the native Celtic Church . . . a matter that was not to be resolved for some centuries. While the Church in Britain and Gaul held to many peculiar practices, defying the political concept of a state Church with firm materialistic ends, the Church in Rome increasingly became an organ of suppression and control. Thus Father Melchior utters a number of obscure heretical prayers and rituals which are either Celtic or Gnostic, and certainly would not have found favour with the Pope. Some of his utterances, incidentally, were preserved in oral tradition in Gaelic-speaking areas well into the eighteenth and nineteenth centuries, and none of them are mere fabrications or fantasies.

The chapel in which the story is told is built from the remains of a stone circle or sanctuary, as was often the case. In this chapel resides a curious relic; a skull is kept and associated with a water ritual. Customs of this sort are recorded in Scotland and Wales as recently as the present century, and a contemporary example of magical therapy in traditions associated with a skull is given by Dr Anne Ross in her book *Folklore of the Scottish Highlands*. The Celtic reverence for the head, and for skulls connected with water and magical practices, is not simply a curiosity from the distant past; it has a deep significance which endures in actual tradition. It conceals and at the same time reveals a profound mystery. In the tale of Peredur certain objects are displayed during a ritual procession in a hall or castle; one of these is a dish containing a severed head. This sequence, with the gradual exclusion of the head in favour of the vessel alone, gradually became the central vision of the later Grail legends . . . yet the head remained in Welsh traditional tales from which the *Mabinogion* known to us today derives.

In the re-telling, the adventures of Peredur are used by the old saint to encourage his pupil to learn about the mystery of the head, to visualise otherworldly locations and beings, and to ponder and meditate upon the role and power of women. In this last context is Peredur's mother who lays a *geas* or binding magical condition upon him regarding arms and armour; it is an otherworldly maiden who initiates him into the subtle arts of what is possibly swordplay; and it is an old hag who finally tells him how to lift the *geas* while battling an adversary of terrifying power and appearance.

These are all typical themes in Celtic lore; they also appear in folklore worldwide, revealing deep insights into human nature and development towards maturity, through magical transpersonal psychology which far predates our modern theories. Such insights were eventually woven into the highly ethical and religious Grail legends in an attenuated but coherent and persistent set of expressions.

Peredur, the Blundering Hero, gains his arms and armour in a conflict with a being from the Underworld, and incidentally learns all about fighting techniques during the encounter. At that point we leave him, though in traditional legend he has many further adventures ahead of him. Our anonymous pupil, listening to the stirring teachings of his aged mentor, finally realises that there is more than one type of warrior and that the battle of the spirit is as essential to the land, and to its people, as the clash of swords and spears.

Many are the ballads and tales concerning Peredur son of Evrawg; during the long winter nights when snow presses on the roof thatch and ice drips from the smoke-hole, men and women are glad indeed to hear of his youthful exploits. But I heard of Peredur and his greatest adventure early one mid-summer morning just at sunrise, from old Father Melchior, in his tiny chapel of great stones and turf, roofed with withies and a golden net of flowers to the light.

First he praised God the Originator of the World, crossing himself many times as he intoned the chant; next he drew aside the altar cloth of richly dyed wool, to reveal a mystery that I had not seen before. The altar was of dark oak, almost black, and carved in the semblance of a man sleeping in a little chamber bed or perhaps in his coffin. Many curious designs and solemn triangular faces surrounded this figure; here was the old earth-woman with her generous organ open for all, men on horses and carrying stout spears, three hooded ones staring out into the church, and a procession which wound around the border of the sleeper, filled with tiny men and women bearing a platter on which a severed head was displayed, and a lance that

24

seemed to fountain drops of fluid upon the company. All of this I saw in an instant, interwoven with leaves, coils, serpents, and complex traceries and maze trails; then Father Melchior opened the breast of the sleeping figure, and putting his hand within, drew out something covered in a pure white cloth embroidered with a cross and flying bird.

I knew that this object could not be the elements of the mass, for they were kept in a hollow in the thick stone block behind the altar, just below the ever-burning lamp with its coiled dragons in bronze and silver, said to have come from Rome, Imperial city. It was as if the father had reached into the sleeper's body and plucked out his heart, and for a foolish moment I expected the old holy man to turn with a bleeding fragment of flesh in his thin hands. The sight of the delicate embroidery calmed my strange imaginings; then Father Melchior deftly eased the cloth to reveal a golden platter holding an aged yellowing skull. I could hardly believe my eyes, and crossed myself several times invoking Saint Brigit with a silent prayer. Hardly had I completed this act when the skull was placed reverently upon the altar, still sitting upon its platter, staring sightlessly to the west and therefore directly toward me.

'This service', said the priest, his back straightening from the bow of age, his weak eyes shining with a sudden fire, 'has been undertaken here in the holy place since before our ancestors came sailing up out of the West. Here, child, is the mystery that may not be broken. . . .' With these words, he stood to one side and let the full light of the early morning strike upon the skull; it reflected in the polished golden dish, and for a moment I saw a great radiance surrounding a face of such unearthly beauty that tears sprang into my eyes. Then it was gone, and I blinked back the water where I had been dazzled by the reflected dawnlight upon the gold.

With slow careful movements, Father Melchior raised a

small earthenware ewer, and gently sprinkled water from the holy well upon the skull. Three times did he spinkle it in the names of the Trinity, three times again in the names of the kings, heroes and bards, and three times again in the names of the Virgin, her mother and her sister. After each sprinkling he carefully wiped the aged bone with a clean linen cloth, and crossed himself three times. Then he uttered the prayer of our Lord, kneeling and remaining in contemplation.

As he knelt I looked upon the skull, looking back at me, where it rested beneath the ornately jewelled and enamelled cross that bore a Wheel atop the Pillar of earth-to-sky. The Saviour had hung upon that Wheel, I knew, but who had once looked out of that skull and what had he known of God or gods or goddesses?

Without further ceremony, the priest turned almost without rising, and sat upon the worn stone altar steps built of three slim huge sarsens laid one upon the other when the chapel was first assembled. The fire in his eyes had dimmed, and he coughed formally. I knew this cough, it was the preliminary to a lesson; I wondered what it might be . . . Jesus and his love for Mary Magdalene, perhaps, or the story-telling contest between the druid and Saint Martinus, or that favourite of Father Melchior's in which the love and forbearance of Joseph the Carpenter were extolled. But it was to be none of these, nor was it to be verses from the Gospel.

'So the kings, heroes and bards are tucked in between the Trinity and the Virgins for their safety, and we can begin our lesson without fear of interruption. Listen while I tell of the adventures of Peredur son of Evrawg, which may not be changed in the re-telling though a thousand times a thousand men summon them upon their tongues. This story holds the secrets of the Blessed Head, the Holy Vessel, and

26

the Quest for Peace. Long before our Saviour came into the human world this tale was known to men who walked in darkness and sought the light; by the power of His angels and archangels is it made at one with His revelation. Long after our Saviour departed for the realms of Summer and left us longing for his return, has the tale been upheld and the service of the Blessed Head celebrated at dawn each midsummer. In the maze of time, shown outwardly upon the traceries of the Cross with its pillar supporting the Wheel, we uphold the promise that our Saviour will come again, Christ the only Druid, returning in beauty, in glory, and in victory, blessing all shadows and transforming them to light. Then, in that last day, and only then, will this service end; but until that day all who undertake it through the years of shadow will be known by the name of Melchior.'

I waited, almost thinking that he had forgotten about the story of Peredur in this ritual preamble; as I waited, I wondered why a tale known in every house and tavern and poorly heated steam-room or ruinous public bath across Britain should be given such a holy circumstance.

'Once there was a lad called Peredur son of Evrawg, seventh son of his noble father who was chieftain of the fortress North. But his war-wise father and lusty blood-stained brothers were killed in battle with the savages, and, thinking to save her last son, Peredur's mother withdrew with a company of women to her maternal estate. He was not trained in arms or riding, or even wrestling, though he was big and bonny and strong like the wind upon the hills or a hawk in the mountains. Instead of fostering him out as was proper, his mother had a house built in the forest, where she surrounded him with a veritable tribe of maidens and woman servants, as if this ploy could keep him from the evils of the world.' At the mention of a tribe of women, Father Melchior crossed himself absent-mindedly. I had heard this

27

tale before, and found it hard to be attentive sitting upon the cold unyielding stone flags of the chapel floor.

'Now Peredur was flushed with youth and powerfully innocent; one morning while out leaping great leaps in the sun, he ran with the herd of goats from his mother's farm, bleating as they did, and prancing to and fro for joy. Soon he outran these fleet caprines and sped onwards into the golden green forest; there he met with three hinds which he mistook for goats without horns, and so he herded the deer, swiftest of the swift and wildest of the wild, back to the goat pen. His mother and her nine maidens were astonished at such speed and strength, while Peredur clapped his hands to see the deer leap over the goat-wall and run away once the truth was explained to him.

'Not long after this Peredur and his mother were sitting at the door of the hall, each before a doorpost, his mother before the red doorpost and Peredur before the gold. In the distance through the trees a flashing light caught their eyes, and as it flashed it drew closer and closer, bobbing up and down. Soon they could see that it was sunlight flashing and reflecting from helmets of gilded and enamelled steel atop the heads of three riders.

'Peredur sat with his jaw dropping like a gate to the Underworld, but his mother frowned and muttered. Each rider wore a fine kilt of supple tooled leather set with iron plates and gilded spiral-patterned studs. Each wore a red leather tunic woven with gold wire threads in the pattern of spiralling serpents, and across their broad chests were black belts fitted with silver and steel rings, bearing short flesh-biting swords sleeping in their engraved scabbards. Each bore two spears, long and short, with inlaid magical patterns upon the blood-drinking blades. As these wondrous riders drew close, Peredur could see that the leader bore a helmet on which a wide-winged bird seemed about to leap up

28

into the blue heavens, so fine were the metal and enamel and flashing jewel eyes. The two riders following this hawk-crowned chieftain wore headgear without bird or beast upon it, but their helmets were brightly polished and worked with inlays and spirals and weavings that made Peredur cross his eyes with strain studying their intricate patterns.'

For a moment, Father Melchior paused and closed his eyes; he knew that he had caught my attention and deliberately waited for me to ask a question; but this teaching game was one that I was beginning to understand, and I restrained myself from asking why he had introduced warriors in their modern dress armour into an ancient bardic tale. With a slight cough of disappointment, he looked at me suddenly, as if to be quite sure that I did not sleep after all. . . .

' "Mother, who are these men?" Peredur cried, in a loud penetrating voice such as youths always have. "They are not men," she muttered crossly, "they are . . . angels. Now be a good boy and run along and play with the pigs for a while, and don't tip the boar on his head again." Peredur knew better than to disobey his mother, and reluctantly left her sitting at the door to welcome the strangers.

'But as every boy knows, Peredur waited until the guests had been welcomed and feasted, until their horses had been fed and watered and rubbed down and re-saddled, and when the guests set off into the late afternoon sun he crept after them through the long tree-shadows. With his grace and speed he ran alongside the startled horses crying, "Greetings, oh angels, what are those long sticks that you carry and why does that hawk sit so still upon your chieftain's head?" And so he amazed the warriors with his speed, his stealth and his stupidity. They dismounted and told him patiently that they were *equites*, which is Roman for horsemen, from the warband of the young King Arthur. They had come upon a mission to bid his noble mother remarry and sulk no longer with her nine maidens in the woods, changing the colour of her dresses every day. But they had little success with such politics, for no man living has yet been able to dictate policy to a Celtic woman. Peredur asked a thousand boyish questions about weapons, horses, and the gathering at Arthur's fortress of Caerleon, and as he seemed a strapping likely lad, though perhaps wanting in wit, they answered patiently before sending him home.

'Thus did he learn about Arthur, his warriors, weaponry, horses, and the bold attempts to bring order to the conflict-torn land of Britain. And of course he ran off home and broke his mother's heart, for nothing would do but riding off to join the warbands just as his father and brothers had done before him. But she laid a *geas* on him that he would not find arms either on earth, under sky, or over water; and being a simple innocent youth he lumbered off to look for something else that might do instead. He took the tattered, haltered old nag used for hauling firewood, and laid a leather bucket, which he squashed flat, over her back as a saddle. He picked up two long-pronged meat-forks from the kitchen, and, as the cook threw an iron pot at him for the theft, stuck this upon his head as a helmet. Then surrounded by wailing women unable to stop him, he rode off after the angels to the gathering of the warriors of Arthur.'

Although I had heard the tale before in the kitchens, or in the high bardic language of the hall before chieftains, Father Melchior filled his telling with curious details, twists and turns, woven as tightly and as mysteriously as the twists and mazy patterns upon the Cross or around the edges of dress armour or a queen's royal robe. The midsummer sun rose high; through the wide-open chapel door the air curled in warm, slow, pollen-filled, gentle breaths. I had risen before dawn, and, with the shock of that strange early service, my two-day fast, and the priest's singsong bardic intonation, I became drowsy. Even as I half-slept I knew enough of the tale of Peredur to catch at the verses where he innocently defends a slandered queen, though Father Melchior cunningly made her into Arthur's own bride, as if the story had happened yesterday and not many lifetimes past. Just as the hero defeated an arrogant disrespectful bully by flipping his fork into the horseman's eye-socket right through his leather mask and on into the brain, I fell over, my forehead striking the moist stone floor. The shock of that tiny fall, and the cool touch of the aged sarsen, laid flat long ago from its upright stance in the druid sanctuary, brought me wide awake in an instant.

Father Melchior looked at me sternly, prepared to wait forever in silence while I suffered the reproach of his watery old eyes. It was certainly time for me to ask an intelligent question. . . .

'Father, why do you warn against women in this story? First the mother of the hero and her maidens, then the insulted queen and . . .'

'That, my child, is a typical error of one who sleeps when he should be awake, eats when he should fast, and daydreams when he should pay strict attention to his tutor. The teaching today is not against women, but against men who see only one aspect of woman. The robust loud-voiced Peredur saw his mother only as a mother; the degraded and insulting robber chief saw the young queen only as a maiden belonging to the king; if you pay close attention in the true mode of priest and poet rather than sleep and grunt like a Roman governor, you will understand certain mysteries. A woman has three aspects, not merely one role, just as the ancient goddesses of Rome and Gaul and Britain were once in triple form, but now are transcended by the Virgin, her Mother, and her Sister.'

Here he muttered a short prayer and crossed himself several times, while I turned my eyes heavenward to seek blessing, and bowed to the altar. On coming upright from my bow I saw the skull, and for a moment it seemed to smile at me in jocular friendly manner from its golden platter in the sunlight. I remembered the gospel story of the Druidess Salome and the mad seer Johannes; perhaps this skull once nodded on the shoulders of some frothing prophet bounding across the moorlands yelping like a wolf. At this wandering thoughtful image I smiled and almost laughed aloud, as if the skull had shared a joke with me, but Father Melchior looked so outraged that I crossed myself several times and sat down abruptly, looking intense and respectful.

'Now Peredur,' continued the priest, 'still wearing his iron cooking pot and carrying his forks bloodied in the service of Arthur Dragon Chief, refused to attend the assembly because of some imagined insult or other from the steward Kei. The two giant blockheads had insulted one another, and thinking to behave in a noble manner (which nowadays means a muddy mockery of both British and Roman civility) Peredur rode off on his stumbling nag, with the queen's favourite table napkin tied lovingly around his arm.

'So it was that he came to a great river, by the side of which lay a lame chieftain or king, grey with age, lined with wisdom. All about this lord were supporters and kinsmen by blood and by marriage, casting nets into the fast clear water and drawing in salmon which leapt high across the foam-flecked rocks. The chieftain reclined upon a rich red golden litter, hung with resplendent curtains of green and white fashioned with images of lilies and royal crowns. By his side were two handsome boys, one with red flame hair and yellow tunic, one with jet black lustrous hair and green tunic. These two played chess upon a marvellous board where the pieces moved of their own accord. The light squares of the board were of purest silver, while the dark squares were of exotic ebony blacker than peat; as for the chessmen, they were of jade inlaid with crystal. Each of the horsemen on the board had two tiny golden spears and bright helmets, but the white king was laid out in a litter while the dark king rode a champing black stallion frothing at a bronze bit and hung with tiny silver skulls about its trappings.

'As Peredur stood gazing in wonder at this assembly, servants ran up to him and begged him in soft pleasant voices to dismount and rest. They took his pot and forks, and stripped the bucket from the nag's back as lovingly as if these were arms made by the fabled Wayland Smith in Segontium. None, however, touched the queen's favour tied about his broad upper arm.

'Soon the lame king, for king he surely was, bade Peredur approach, asking him if he played the game of chess. "Alas," cried the youth in his loud penetrating voice, combined of piping treble and gruff bass in most unharmonious mis-union, "I do not know the steps of this tiny dance at all, though perhaps I could learn. How do the little men and women cross from black to white and white to black squares of their own accord with no hand to guide them from above?" The two boys, green and yellow, looked at one another and smiled.

' "I see from your mark of favour," said the king, changing the subject as civilised manners require when a guest displays folly, "that you have already fought honourably and victoriously for the blessing of a woman. Judging by the stains of gravy and honey and the quality of the woven linen, I would say that she must be a queen at least. It is our custom to welcome nobles such as yourself to a feast and to a night of rest in the hall wherein I rule, and all of my line have ruled since the Creator laid out the Four Beginnings beyond the summer stars."

'And without further glance or words, the king signalled to his company by striking a tiny silver gong. Immediately they drew in their nets, and evening came on; bearing the golden bed upon their shoulders his body servants stood upright and tall, while his runners and ghillies blew horns and shouted and hallooed shrilly; the two youths picked up the chessboard and marvellous game pieces and marched along boldly, while riding bards upon white horses plucked harps and sang, and pages bearing long silken banners marked with lilies and golden crowns strutted and stumbled behind, pausing to hitch up their kilts at every few steps. Thus they all processed by the broad shining river into a dark shadowy forest as night fell. As they passed beneath great oak trees, the last rays of the sun touched the branches, and it seemed to Peredur that he passed beneath a tree half of green leaves and half of living burning flame. Then they were on a shadowed forest path, winding through the ferns, with the runners singing softly to the muted harps of the bards, tuned to that evening scale beloved of all Britons.

'At length they came to a level meadow lit not by sun or moon but by the light streaming from the open doors of a great hall set upon pale silver grass. Each pillar of that door was seven times the height of a man, and carven like an ancient giant such as walked the world in former times. One giant bore a surly sneering snarling face, and the other a happy smiling jovial face. So vast was that hall that the runners and ghillies and horsemen and fishers and boys and pages with banners and bards with harps and lads with whips and hounds wearing bronze collars studded with green and blue glass all passed straight in without pause or confusion. In the porch, the company all dismounted and stable boys took the horses and hound masters took the great hounds and mastiffs, coaxing them with raw meat, and scullions rushed up from the kitchens below to snatch away the bag of salmon fresh from the river.

'Peredur looked around him, turning in a slow circle, his jaw hanging slack and his bright blue eyes goggling; the porch alone could have held Arthur's hall at Caerleon or the camp at Camelodunum, or both at once. Through the towering pillars that upheld the distant roof, each pillar shaped like a different kind of tree in its prime and glory, Peredur could see a variety of halls, rooms, passages, chambers, galleries, baths, vaults, stairs, columns, arches, and pleasant walkways filled with singing birds. Some were of rich carven wood, some of rough or hewn stone, others had walls of glowing crystal, while a few were of brightly burnished metal that looked fresh out of the furnace.

'The two boys of green and yellow tunics, red and jet black hair, led Peredur, entranced, taking him by either hand and drawing him gently towards an inner hall. Never had he been more self-conscious, never had he been so aware of his boorish lack of manners or courtly civilized style and grace; bemused and confused as he was, Peredur made a strong silent vow to follow the teachings of his wily old nurse, and to hold his tongue whatever he might chance to hear or see in that place.

'At the doorway to the inner hall, Peredur was met by the steward who gave him bread and salt, and a bowl of silver engraved with stags leaping and filled to the brim with clear water to bathe his filthy feet. Thus he became a sacred guest in that mysterious place, and all unknowing took bonds upon himself that no man may loose without great daring joy and terror.

'When he had washed, a most beautiful young maiden wearing a gown of spring green woven with bright yellow daffodils came up to Peredur, and lightly touching his arm said: "Chieftain, for such I take you to be by your great size and vigour, it is the custom of this hall that any guest shall be

35

obliged to strike a blow at my request. Can you use a sword?"

' "I could," answered Peredur as he blushed hotly at her touch, "if I had instruction, but I have had none. Besides, my mother laid this *geas* upon me that I shall not have arms or armour either on earth, under sky, or over water." At this the maiden frowned, and gazed earnestly into the youth's sweaty face. "Nevertheless," she murmured, "you can bear the sword that I request, for here you are neither on earth, under sky, nor are you over sea. But you will not be able to bear this sword when you leave me, and the lifting of a mother's curse must be done alone and unaided."

'Then she took Peredur by the hand, which made him tremble and think that the hall was too hot for the time of year, and led him to a huge stone column rising up in the middle of the place. Resting beneath the stone was a long black iron sword singing and humming to itself with power. "Take the sword," said the maiden, "and strike a blow at the stone."

'So Peredur picked up the sword, which moaned and writhed at his touch, and, striking a great blow at the stone, cut it into two parts; and the sword also shattered into two and stopped murmuring. But the maiden came and joined the stone together with a pass of her gentle hands, and likewise fused the sword as new by stroking it. A second time she bid him strike, and again he broke both sword and pillar. She gently joined the stone and revived the sword again, and bid him strike home with a will. And on this third stroke both sword and stone flew apart from one another and could not be joined together.

' "Well struck indeed," murmured the maiden. "And now I hear my father calling to bid us to the feast." At this the sound of a silver gong rang through every chamber and hall, and they passed into a place lit with great crystals and silver lamps in the shape of serpents. There was a feast laid out upon groaning oaken boards, and all men and women served one another equally of the abundant food and wine and none sat above the other or had precedence of gifts or rich couches.

'Peredur sat on one side of the king and the maiden upon the other; pleasant was the conversation in that hall, and they laughed and talked in high spirits for many hours. But as the feast drew to a close, the two lads of green and yellow entered from a long dark doorway in the shadows; they carried between them a huge spear so fierce that it seemed to draw them forward rather than be supported by their hands. From the sharp blade set in a stout socket there spurted three streams of blood running and flowing over the floor of the feasting hall. Peredur longed to know the meaning of this mystery, but held his tongue just as his nurse had taught him. The assembled company set up a wailing and crying and ululating such as would break a man's heart with grief and sorrow and longing, until Peredur, clutching his tongue with his right hand, could hardly bear to be in that place another moment.

'As the lamenting died away, there was a moment of deep silence, and two immaculate young girls appeared robed in purest white. They bore between them a large platter upon which was set the severed head of a man, gory with clots of blood and horrible with white upturned eyes and matted locks of dark hair. Again the company mourned aloud, and this time Peredur almost bit through his fingers.

'No one spoke a word after this procession had passed, and all seemed lost in a strange languorous trance. Presently a boy servant crept up to Peredur and signed silently that he should follow; thus did the warrior of pot and forks find his sleeping cubicle for that silent and portentous night.

'When Peredur awoke from his deep youthful sleep, a

servant brought him warm scented water in which to dip his head and a cup of wine mixed with honey and mint. He stumbled out into the great hall, and found the lame king sitting upon a royal throne with the two youths wrestling at his feet. First one youth would seem to gain the upper hand, then the other, but neither the yellow nor the green could make a winning throw.

' "Which of these two combatants do you consider more strong?" asked the old king. "Perhaps . . . the green one?" Peredur answered uncertainly. "But in truth I cannot tell." "Then try to throw him upon the ground," the king replied gravely.

'Peredur lumbered up to the dark-haired youth in the green tunic, who smiled sweetly at him. After great effort and struggling Peredur overthrew this youth by the fall known as "Jacob's Angel" which he found quite by accident before the kingly throne. As the youth fell, the great hall shook and trembled and the flames in the lamps guttered and dimmed for an instant just as day broke in the land of Britain.

'When he rose from this uncouth sport, Peredur saw the lovely maiden coming towards him where he stood by her father's throne. Her golden and silver mantles shone like the sun and her face was like the light of many stars blessing the radiant moon. Greatly daring, Peredur ventured to greet her, but she would have none of such greetings.

' "Greeting I will not give you, not in the British manner or the Roman," she cried, "for though you are great of strength, you are lacking in wit. What manner of man are you that passes his first test, fails the second, yet passes the third? Because of your silence in the hall of feasting and sorrow, you shall get no welcome from me. But because of your lucky wrestling fall, you may look for me again when you have arms and armour and are freed from your mother's curse." And with these strange bitter words and hidden promise, she turned and strode off down one of the long glittering galleries of that place.

'Peredur was confused and ashamed; he turned to the old lame king, but he was nodding as if asleep; he turned to the two youths, but they were now deep into a game of chess and not to be disturbed. So he turned again to seek his way out of the hall and back to the court of Arthur where the rules of conduct were more direct and simple. As he turned, he wondered how he might find arms and armour and be free of his mother's *geas* . . . and if the maiden really would welcome him again upon such freedom.

'In the great porch, his heart heavy and his mind dull, his body aching from the wrestling match, Peredur waited while servants brought out his nag, neatly groomed, and his well-polished bucket, pot, and forks. As he mounted he heard a wild cackling sound of laughter from behind the doorpost. Leering out at him was a withered filthy old crone; she had a wrinkled warty face, cross-grown brown and black teeth, snarling loose lips, gum-seeping red rimmed eyes, and a hunched back. This hag wore a threadbare black robe stained with old blood and egg yolks and grey powdery scum; she clenched and unclenched her grimy brown hands, bulging with blue veins and sporting horn-yellow earth-filled nails that twisted into long spirals and hooks.

' "Oh my, what a thick-headed buffoon you are," she croaked, sidling crabwise towards him. "Your grandfather must have been a legionary man or tax collector . . . but for a small gift I will tell you where you can find arms and armour that will lift your mother's curse in an instant, but you'll have to jump for it, mark my words. Well, bonny boy, what do you say?"

'Peredur was shocked at this apparition and her candid domineering manner of speech, but he knew that the ancient British code of honour demanded total respect to all women, for this much had his mother and his old nurse taught him from the cradle onwards.

' "I would willingly give you a gift, granny," he replied courteously. "But I have nothing worth giving. My strength comes from God and my lineage and is not my own to give. I am lacking in all skills, save perhaps striking blows and wrestling, and am cursed to bear no leather tunic, arms or armour, which are the very substance of a warrior's life. And above all this I have foolishly offended my host and his daughter, simply by holding my tongue as my old nurse taught me to do so well."

' "Well spoken, lad," the crone cackled and croaked. "You are beginning to wake up at last. Well spoken indeed . . . how many men truly know what is and is not theirs to give? How many men know when they have spoken rightly or wrongly or failed to speak? You are doing well, and in return for your progress, I shall only ask you for a little kiss. Come down off that poor feeble horse, and give me a little kiss, right here upon the mouth." And she pointed with her grimy nailed finger to her livid twisting mottled lips where her crossed rotting teeth stuck out like fangs.

'Now Peredur had learned from his nurse and his mother and the nine maidens in his mother's house that a woman's request was usually a command. He knew which requests could be flouted, and which were to be obeyed no matter how lightly they were uttered. So although he would rather have kissed the daughter of the king, he approached the hag and embraced her gently, closing his eyes. She stank of rotting meat and stale beer; she felt like a bag of putrid bones slithering around in his arms. Her breath was rich with garlic, wormwood, feverfew, vervain and yeasty fungus, while her stomach rumbled like a river underground. As he kissed her, she gently stroked his hair for a moment, then suddenly grabbed it tight in her fist and jerked hard. "Listen to me, little hero, go as fast as you can out of this forest and seek the great mound that lies upon its border. Climb the mound and you will find a tree, and beneath the tree you will find a stone. Blow the horn that rests at the foot of that stone three times, and fight whoever appears for the possession of his arms and armour." Then she boxed his ears hard, pushed him and his nag out of the great porch to the king's hall, and slammed the huge bronze-plated iron-studded doors behind him. "And remember to jump ..." she screamed as the doors ground clashing together.

'With aching ears and burning scalp, Peredur plodded off down the ferny path, leading his tired old horse. When he came to the border of the great forest, he espied a mound rearing up to the sky, right between tree shadows and meadow sunlight. It was just as the crone had said, for standing upon the summit of this mound was a little gnarled hawthorn tree, beneath which stood an ancient Druid stone. Peredur climbed the mound and picked up the plain hunting horn that lay by the stone. Capping his iron pot tightly over his head, gripping his two cooking forks firmly in his right hand, Peredur summoned up his courage and blew both loud and shrill.

'With the first blast, clouds scurried over the sun and grey sorrowful light filled the sky; with the second blast, hail and rain fell from above the mound in a stinging torrent that stripped the leaves from the hawthorn tree ... a great scurrying and running and galloping of creatures could be heard all around, though nothing could Peredur see but a sheet of falling icy water. With the third blast, the earth heaved up, and out of the mound reared a huge black man with one eye and one arm and one leg, wearing ancient rusty armour and bearing a huge spear and sword and long triple shield. Shedding soil and rocks from his head and

41

shoulders, he towered over Peredur and his single eye blazed bright green with battle frenzy.

'All that day they fought, and the fight was equal yet unequal, for Peredur had never been in a true battle before with anyone larger than himself and more skilled, yet he learned so quickly that he copied every move that the warrior made. Every jink and jump, twist and turn, thrust and parry, Peredur copied, and by sunset he had many slight wounds, but had learned all of the warrior's subtle art. Not once had he touched the black man with his fork, and not once had he closed in to wrestle him; nor had the giant struck a deadly blow upon Peredur, for always the youth leapt beyond the full strike of his sword, or ducked beneath the length of the spear.

'As darkness drew on, the warrior of the mound seemed to grow in size and move with greater speed; Peredur hurled both his forks with all his strength and saw them strike home, yet no harm came to his adversary. Just as the one-legged one-armed warrior raised his terrible flesh-cutting sword to strike, Peredur remembered the words of the old hag who had sent him to this place, and leapt high off the earth to land hard upon the black warrior's head. As he struck there was a great clap of thunder, and the tree was struck and the stone shattered. The warrior vanished and Peredur crashed hard to the ground.

'He awoke to find himself atop the mound at night, with summer stars shining brightly overhead. Both tree and stone stood whole, as if he had dreamed of their destruction; but by his side was a full set of black leather and iron armour, a sharp sword, and a crested helmet with no less than two eagles flying from its crown.'

At last Father Melchior paused, and I sat in astonishment, thrilled by this heroic ending, but bursting with questions.

'Father, why did the hero . . .', but he laid his hand upon my mouth in the ancient sign for silence used in holy places since the world was young.

'But the crone was . . .'. Again the priest made the sign upon my mouth, and even as I drew in breath, he made it a third time, which was utterly binding upon any man, even a king. I knew that I was meant to meditate upon the questions that I longed to ask and upon the many deep meanings hidden in the old tale and the changes that the father had made in his curious re-telling. How were the women in the tale connected? What were the questions that Peredur failed to ask? What was the meaning of the sword and stone, mysterious procession, and the wrestling bout? Who was the dark warrior in the mound upon the borderlands? One thing at least I knew; that battle had occurred on an ancient mound between the otherworld of the lame king and the human world of Arthur and his chieftains; thus could Peredur lift his mother's curse by leaping high in the air and being free of all bonds. But the rest was beyond my skill; never had I heard such hard riddles woven into a story.

Father Melchior stood and stretched a little, discreetly as befits a teacher before his pupil or a saint before his acolyte. Then he crossed himself several times uttering the formula of the Breastplate of Light, and, lifting the old skull upon its platter, covered it with the cloth. Bending slowly, showing fatigue after the long telling, the priest touched his lips lightly to the covered relic, and replaced it in the secret chamber within the carved sleeping figure's breast. Then he drew the altar cloth over the carving, and knelt to pray, his eyes uplifted to the Cross. He did not summon me to the altar, and I knew that he uttered some silent personal petition to Christ who had hung upon the Wheel and summoned our Ancestors to paradise when he walked across the worlds between the worlds.

As for me, at that moment I suddenly longed to be Peredur, or any brave warrior gaining his arms; I wished that I had a supple leather tunic and sharp bright sword, or scale armour of steel and gold rings woven together and long and short spears; I would ride off to pledge service to the young King Arthur who even now assembled the chieftains and the land owners together to push back the invading savages from the north and the east and the seaways around the land of Britain.

Now Father Melchior motioned that I join him in prayer before the altar. Together we recited the Hymn of the Dancer which the Saviour had taught his beloved company, and the Devotion of the Two Vessels by which faith is embodied, and the Prayer of our Lord which is always heard in every world no matter where the supplicant may be wandering. Finally we intoned the Keystone of the Arch of Heaven, and remained in silent contemplation of the marvellous promise that God has made to Man, signified even today by the mystery of the rainbow that comes and goes without foreknowledge on our part.

Long night shadows filled the ancient chapel; the little dragon lamp from Rome radiated a firm gentle light against the darkness that threatened the land. As I meditated, my imagination was filled with pictures of Peredur, his leaping, his shouting, his strange mother and her nine maidens, the princess who had shown him how to strike with a will, and the hag who had kissed him and lifted his curse by sending him to a place that was no place.

Last of all, my mind returned to the truth of my own lame twisted leg, and the bones that could not be reset. I would never ride with Arthur's war bands, never see the glory of distant Rome. But in that sudden plunging of despair, I felt the stirring of a new understanding, something that I could barely grasp, fused out of the strange experiences of this midsummer day ritual. I began to see the purpose of my lessons from the aged saint who had taken me in when all others cast me aside as useless; I knew that there was more than one kind of service to the land of Britain, and that I too would become Melchior.

The Abduction & Rescue
of Gwenhwyfar the Queen

ONE OF THE most famous and well-known stories in the Arthurian cycle deals with the kidnapping and rescue of Arthur's queen. Chrétien de Troyes made of it his first great foray into the world of Camelot in his *Knight of the Cart*, where it is Lancelot who has the task of rescuing his lady from the evil Meleagraunce. The same story is told, in short form, by Malory. But it is to an earlier version than either of these, which is to be found in the *Life of Gildas*, written by Caradoc of Lancarven in 1150, that we turn for inspiration in our version.

Here, as seems more likely, Arthur is the hero, ranged against a wily, slightly sinister adversary. In Caradoc's tale it is the Saint himself who intervenes to bring about the release of the Queen, but for the purposes of this story Arthur himself must recover his wife unaided – though in the end it is Guinevere (Gwenhwyfar) who solves the impasse with a ploy borrowed from the Welsh story of Trystan and Essyllt (Isolt).

By placing Arthur at centre stage, we realise just how far things changed between the original events of the sixth century and the fanciful stories of the Middle Ages. There Arthur is little more than a figurehead, the central point about which the legends and fables constellate.

So, too, in pushing the whole story further back in time, we find some interesting things happening to the other protagonists in the tale. Sir Kay, for example, the braggart and buffoon of the later stories, becomes again Kei, a redoubtable hero who stands close to Arthur himself; and Melwas, the arch-villain, becomes again Melwas of the Summer Country, an ancient name for the Otherworld as understood by the Celtic people.

The story itself, of the abduction and rescue of the Queen, also dates back many millennia before the time of Arthur. It is indeed a form of a well-known folk-loric motif known as the 'Abduction of the Flower-Bride'. Guinevere herself, like Blodeuwedd in the Mabinogi of *Math, Son of Mathonwy*, can be clearly identified with an otherworldly figure created by magical means.

This may account for the rather unfavourable light in which Arthur's queen appears to be held in many of the stories. She should, given the times, have stood for the figure of *amour courtoise*. Instead we find a rather unsympathetic tone to many of her biographies – probably because many were written by clerics, who could hardly come out in favour of adultery.

Malory's portrait is, as ever, the most psychologically interesting, but the most one can say about the final impression of Guinevere's character is to quote the famous schoolgirl's answer to a question about Arthur's queen, that she was 'a lady much given to being run off with'.

It is said that the wife of the warrior Arthur, she that was named Gwenhwyfar, was the daughter of a giant and that Arthur won her only after terrible slaughter and on the death of her father. As to that – well, I do not know if it is true or not, but I have also heard that he met with a lady in the deep wood and that he bedded her on the grassy floor.

Thereafter he brought her with him back to his stronghold at Camulodunum and made her his wife. And it is whispered – though none speak it openly – that she was of the Elvish kind and not of mortal stock, but that when Arthur married her he married the land, for she was the outward sign of the sovereignty of the realm, and brought with her the gift of the apple-tree that never dies and always bears fruit.

But be that as it may, the tale I would tell you now concerns another time, when Arthur was older – though years seemed not to have marked his queen – when the land was for the most part at peace. Then there came to Camulodunum a hero named Melwas, who named himself King of the Summer Country (though all who heard him speak thus made the sign of the horns against ill luck). But he seemed no more than a man for all that, and it is said that the women he bedded found no fault with him in that way. And so he came to be accepted among the war-band and men soon forgot that he had claimed a title beyond their understanding, and took him for one no different from themselves.

But all the while, he cast looks of longing and desire towards the Lady Gwenhwyfar, and when she would not return them he grew bold and maddened, so that one day it was found that the Queen was missing (though none knew how she had been spirited away) and after that it was found that Melwas was also gone – from which it did not take long to surmise who the two riders leaving Camulodunum strangely muffled in cloak and hood had been who had been seen before daylight, heading west towards the Summer Country.

At once Arthur mustered the war-band and set forth in pursuit, though many muttered that such a course could lead to no good and that the way ahead would soon leave this world behind. Only Gwalchmai and Lugh (who were said to love the Lady Gwenhwyfar equally) refrained from questioning their Lord, and because of this Cei and Bedwyr, Cador and Ydol also kept silence and hastened to keep pace with their grim lord who drove his mount hard from the anger that raged within him.

And for a while the way was easy and the trail not hard to follow, but in a while the character of the land changed, and there were less places that men knew from hunting there, and soon these were gone also, and the war-band rode through a dim world which seemed scarcely there at all, at which many were seen to cast looks of apprehension over their right shoulders, while others kept their faces between their horses' ears and looked neither right nor left.

Now whether they rode into the Otherworld I cannot say, but after they had followed that road for no longer than it would take to cover eight leagues from Camulodunum, they were in a place unfamiliar to any one among them. Where there should have been trees on either hand there were fields of standing corn, and though it seemed past the mid-point of the day, yet the sun stood still in the sky and burned down upon the warriors until they began to tire and their mounts to stumble beneath them. And then at last Arthur called a halt, and looking at them grimly said that he required none to follow him that were afraid of that place, but that he would go forward alone if need be while they waited his return. There were those who felt mindful to remain there, but when they fell to thinking of how it would be to be lost in that place without their leader they all pressed to be allowed to go where Arthur went. And without a word he lead the way onward, seeming to know where he should go.

And sure enough, before long there was the gleam of sunlight on water, and the war-band came to a place of creeks and narrow water-ways surrounded by great reedbeds that seemed alive with birds of many kinds; and there in the centre of that strange, shifting landscape, was a hall of wood, ornately carved, with a ring of sharpened stakes set round it and a gate firmly barred. And Arthur rode up to it, with Lugh and Gwalchmai, Bedwyr and Cei at his back, and set up a cry that made all the birds on the margins of the water-ways rise into the air on sudden wings. And the cry was to Melwas to come forth.

Soon enough the head of the Lord of the Summer Country appeared above the row of sharp spikes and looked down upon the warriors of Arthur, and laughed aloud to see them there.

'Melwas, you have my wife,' said Arthur with iron in his voice. 'Give her up or pay the price with your life.'

'I think not, Arthur,' Melwas answered. 'You have no power here unless I give you leave; only thus have you come so far,' and he raised a hand and spoke words of command whereat one half of the war-band found themselves unable to move either hand or foot, and then all knew for certain (if any still doubted it) that Melwas was no ordinary man. But Arthur did not cease from looking at Melwas, eye to eye, and he said, 'This quarrel is between you and I, Melwas of the Summer Country. Let you come forth and we will settle it man to man.'

But Melwas only laughed and said, 'Since I am not a man, that would be no contest; but if you, or one among you will offer to meet my champion, then it shall be decided thus which one of us will keep your queen.'

Lugh and Gwalchmai would both have spoken then, but Arthur held up his hand and said, 'I alone shall answer this challenge,' and he got down from his grey steed and drew the sword Caledfwlch, that men say was given to him by the goddess of the lake, and set himself ready to meet whatever might come.

Presently the gate of Melwas' stronghold opened and there came forth a fierce and terrible warrior, a span taller than any there. He was tattooed all over with spiral patterns, and carried a great axe in his hands; and many there were who deemed him kin to the Great Gnome with whom Gwalchmai played the Beheading Game and won; and even Lugh of the Strong Arm drew back a pace when he saw the size of the warrior. But Arthur merely smiled and said: 'This one has need of cutting down to size,' and he went forward unafraid.

Of that combat men tell many tales that are even longer in the telling than this whole adventure; therefore I will say only that it lasted throughout all the long hours of the afternoon and at the end of it the grass was stained red with blood and the breaths of the two warriors came harsh and heavy. But neither might find advantage over the other; for while Melwas' champion had the strength of ten men and the swiftness of the Otherworld about his movements, Arthur was guarded by the power of his sword. And so at last Melwas himself appeared in the gateway and bade them stop, and then he summoned his followers within to bring forth the Lady Gwenhwyfar, and said that she might settle this dispute between them, for no other way was there that the matter could end, unless it be in bloody battle or dark enchantment.

And Gwenhwyfar, whom none might look upon without loving her for the beauty and gentleness of her appearance, took thought how best to mend this sorry matter. And at the end she spoke thus (and let it be known that those who say these words were spoken of the woman Iscult and her lover Drystan, that they are liars):

'Let this be the judgement between Arthur and Melwas; that I shall be with one while the leaves are upon the trees and with the other while they are not, and to this both must agree.'

Then Arthur and Melwas looked long at each other and Gwenhwyfar, and so it was agreed between them both; and Melwas spoke first and said that he would have her while there were no leaves on the trees (for he deemed that then the nights would be longest). And Arthur laughed and said: 'Holly and ivy and yew keep their leaves until death; you have lost, Melwas, my queen is restored to me.'

And for that his given word was binding, Melwas gave up the Lady Gwenhwyfar, though he did so with ill grace; and the war-band found that movement was restored to them, and so they left that place and returned to Camulodunum, which seemed but a short ride after all from the Summer Country. But it is said that, afterwards, Lugh of the Strong Arm returned there and slew Melwas – but there are many tales told of Arthur's greatest warrior and I am unable to say which are true and which are not.

Kei & the Giant

THIS TALE, DELIBERATELY short for reasons revealed by the story-teller himself, encompasses a number of themes that run through Celtic and Arthurian legends in their more primitive or primal variants. Kei is a magical warrior in the oldest versions of his adventures; by the medieval period he begins to be rationalised as the steward or even the butler of Arthur's court. This gradual change does not, however, totally disguise his magical nature:

So Kei went to the kitchen and the mead cellar and returned with a jug of mead and a golden cup, and his hands held skewers full of chopped meat. They took the chops and drank the mead, and then Kei said 'Let me have my story as you promised . . .'
(The Countess of the Fountain, The Mabinogion)

Stewardship has a significance which modern readers often miss, especially when Kei or Kay is shown giving out food and drink as in the quote above. In fact he is a guardian figure; a steward is one who oversees the operation of the king's household and therefore the smooth running of the land itself. In his most ancient forms he is an aspect of a god-form, known to the Romans as Janus, the guardian of gateways; in Arthurian tales Kei often has the keeping of the gate to Arthur's court and may refuse or admit as he wills. The significance of stewardship is shown by the historical fact that the Stuart kings of Scotland and then Britain were originally *stewards* to the royal house ... they eventually became kings in their own right when the earlier Scottish line died out in 1371, and Robert the seventh high steward became King Robert II, first of the Steward or Stewart dynasty. The importance of this office is reflected in the medieval description of Kei riding into battle, where, like the historical high stewards of Scotland, his place within the army is second only to that of the king himself:

... the men at the edge of the host were running to the centre and the men at the centre were running to the edge. A rider arrived armed in mail with rings as white as lilies and rivets as red as the reddest blood, and this rider careered through the host ... 'the rider you see is Kei, the most handsome man in Arthur's kingdom. The men at the edge of the host are rushing to the centre to see Kei riding, while the men at the centre are fleeing to the edge to avoid being trampled by his horse.'

(*The Dream of Rhonabwy*, The Mabinogion)

Clearly, even in this late description, Kei is a man of great power. Nor is this description mere flattery, for it reveals the ancient power of polarity, or attraction and repulsion, inherent in the guardian figure. The Arthurian host seethes about Kei the steward, moving in and out around his central power.

But this is the most sophisticated expression of Kei as a magical warrior, tied to the medieval role of high stewardship. The primal guardian is a being of prodigious strength; he can grow to giant size and generate heat; but he is not sinister or anti-human, no matter how violent he may become at times. He is an echo of an Otherworld being or hero, but in the service of kingship and the land.

If he is my son he will be stubborn, whenever he carries a burden great or small it will be visible neither from before or behind; no one will brave fire or water as well as he, nor will there be any steward or officer like him . . .

(Kynyr Elegant Beard speaks of Kei in Culhwch and Olwen,
The Mabinogion)

He had this talent; nine days and nights he could hold his breath under water, nine days and nights he could go without sleep. No doctor could cure a wound from his sword . . . he could be as tall as the tallest tree in the forest, and his hands generated heat for the kindling of fires.

(Description of Kei in Culhwch and Olwen)

Kei is found in the following tale in this early or primal form; he is a giant who changes shape and challenges the titanic powers of nature, the world, even the stars. He is also a humorous character, and this is very important indeed. The beneficial giant/heroes are often subjects of humour or ridicule, even at the height of their great adventures which confer benefit upon all of humankind.

The contest of giants is an enduring mythological theme found worldwide; Kei is the giant warrior who links the human world or tribal world to the Otherworld, while his adversary is a giant of a quite different type who spans the starry heavens.

As so many elements of the primal Kei character suggest a myth, it seems fitting that he should fight the battle that reflects the relationship between humans and environment, seasonal patterns, weather lore, and ultimately the pattern of the cosmos. His adversary is the giant Orion, the most terrifying hunter ever known. This constellation, with that of the Pleiades, played an important role in seasonal and astronomical/religious calenders in the ancient world. On the most simple level, sailing seasons were defined by these constellations, as were the turning points of the agricultural year; Kei therefore becomes a hero standing at the centre of the world (shown by Arthur's court) and perceiving the mysteries of the seasons and the four cardinal directions.

Thus Kei, the guardian of Arthur's court, has a battle of prodigious nature . . . or as it turns out is willing to enter into such a battle, but his adversary is so vast that he is almost beyond reach. Kei also unwittingly maps out the world by his grumbling comments upon weather; ordered patterns of 'world-making' were important to Celtic culture, mystical cosmologies were shown forth as actual geography and social relationships. We know from historical literary sources that Irish kingdoms were divided according to geographical/ cosmological plans with highly defined social castes and roles allocated to certain areas or directions.

A fourfold pattern, connected to the Four Elements and the Seasons, was central to both religion and philosophy in the ancient world, and certainly had prominence in the sixth century in Britain, as both poetry and archaeological remains show. This pattern was perpetuated right through the Middle Ages and on into the eighteenth and even nineteenth centuries; it still persists today as the foundation for modern magical arts and astrology. The origins of this worldview are rooted in observation of the weather and of the stars, and in various ancient and enduring practices of meditation and religion.

So a silly tale about a ludicrous giant who clubs oxen to death with his bare fists and boorishly challenges the stars themselves to battle can lead us, as with so many Arthurian themes, into the most elemental mysteries. Kei's adventure on the roof of Arthur's hall (which is of course the centre of the world!) stops short just as he is about to reach into the star-world above. Such visions persisted in medieval texts such as the *Prophecies and Life of Merlin* in which Celtic,

Greek, and encyclopedic knowledge were fused together under the unifying figure of the British prophet. If the reader wishes to know what Kei might have seen in the stars, the answer is found in those two books.

It is well known, at least among civilised people, that King Arthur's steward Kei was big. But you must understand that the size of Kei was changeable; at one time as tall as an oak tree, at another merely the height of the rooftop but broad as a wine butt. This too is an understanding that comes to people of culture rather than to barbarians.

On the subject of Size, and the essential brother of Size who is of course Strength, we must pause and reflect. It is frequently given out in songs and tales that Kei grew, or shrank; sometimes roaring like a full angry river in spate, sometimes merely rumbling like a millstone grinding on a quiet summer evening . . . heard for miles around but not threatening in tone. There are certain judgements upon this matter of Size and Strength, civilised comparisons that may be made, for a savage sees such forces in a very different way to a man of culture, tradition and wisdom.

Without further preamble or ado, therefore, we must be aware that Kei was no bigger (most of the time) than any healthy champion. His appetite for beef was no greater than that of any hero; his capacity for wine no more cavernous than any truly civilised person remote from barbarism. But there are certain facts worthy of your attention; firstly men are smaller nowadays than were their ancestors. The mighty men of old were indeed of a stature greater than the weaklings of today; secondly all measures of height, breadth, depth, or of bread, meat, wine, weapons and the like, have not diminished in proportion to the size of men. Thus a six-foot sword is still a six-foot sword and a gallon of mead still a gallon; but the man that swings the blade after drinking the gallon is more likely to cut his own head off than to think of it as light exercise after a refreshing tipple.

Thirdly, and most important of all, barbarians are, or were, inevitably smaller than civilised men. This diminution of the savage was due to his poor diet, his wearing of restrictive uniform clothing, his collective habit of marching up and down in tight clumps of regular numbers, and his housing within stone boxes devoid of air and healthy rainfall. In short, if you will excuse my pun, the Romans were squat and weak while our ancestors were tall and strong. Indeed, there are weak-minded sycophants who will argue to the contrary; would-be inheritors of land ownership or exotic detractors from simple ancestral values, but the historical facts speak loudly for themselves.

A proof? You want proof; very well. If anyone doubts my words, let him go to the remains of Caerleon or Chester or Aquae Sulis, and examine in details the remains of the buildings and the content of the inscriptions upon the stones. He will find from the inscriptions that the men stationed in these places or visiting the temples to worship were all members of ancestral Celtic tribes, or even distant cousins from far Sarmatia or Russia; their own names and messages still visible today confirm this fact. Then let the doubting researcher measure accurately the size of the buildings that remain or the breadth of the foundations of the ruins; he will soon realise just how tall those ancestors of ours really were, and why the dwarfish meagre degenerate Romans enlisted them to strengthen the enervated Legions of the Empire. Then let our diligent scholar travel if he will to Rome itself, or what is left of it, and discover that the Celtic soldiers of the mad Emperors were of such a height that vast colonnades, circuses, roadways and tall overleaning buildings were constructed to accommodate them.

The size of Kei undoubtedly was of ancestral order;

60

normal to his civilised fellow warriors, but enormous to squat, flour-fed, leather-wrapped, hob-nail-sandalled Romans.

Ah . . . what about the Giant? The Giant, I hear you mutter; Kei and the Giant? Well, that is not hard to answer: it goes thus.

One New Year's Day, by the true Celtic Church calendar, and not that of the Roman Church which is merely an unruly offshoot, Kei was butchering an ox for supper. First he killed the ox by thumping it upon the head with his fist, then he plucked out the tongue by the roots; next he squeezed out its eyes and ripped . . . what? Ah, indeed, the Giant. I was coming to that shortly.

Well, as Kei hung the freshly butchered ox over the fire to roast, he tripped upon the rim of the great iron pot that stood by the side of the fire-pit. In so tripping he fell full-length, landing with his face in the warm porridge left over from that morning's breakfast . . . Such a splash did he make that this porridge still falls as frozen flakes each winter; and that was how the first snow fell in Britain, for before that there was only healthy rain and wind.

But with his head under the washing turbulent waves of lukewarm porridge, Kei did not see a long well-muscled silver arm reach down through the smokehole of the roof and snatch away the still quivering barely seared ox. When Kei finally stood up, lifting the pot from off his head and licking the porridge from his beard, no ox could he find. He looked into the flames and sang this song:

> Little flea, little flea
> you hopped in my coat,
> you were not a cat or a dog
> or a goat,
> You fit not a spoon nor a shoe
> nor a box,

But you fit in my glove
the size of an ...

But of course he did not sing the last word as this would reach the ears of the thief who would then know that he was being sung against and hunted. This is the origin of the expression 'a flea in your ear' and of course the phrase 'to box his ears'.

All the women who worked around King Arthur's house and hall very much admired the song that Kei had made, and began to sing out 'Little flea, little flea ...' until everyone in the region knew it so well that they mimicked the creatures in the song, sitting like cats in a spoon, barking like dogs in a shoe, and being stubborn as a goat who will not go into her box at night. And this was the first theatre show in all of Britain, though not the last.

Now Kei was angry at the loss of the flea; his shoulders flexed and his neck stretched, he drew in a great deep breath filled with smoke and song and falling porridge, and he thrust his head right up through the smoke-hole of the roof. The cooking fire was ground out by his feet and the glowing sparks flew up to singe his knees; his great broad shoulders fitted snugly into the roofbeams and his wide throbbing neck filled the central hole to bursting point; the four great winds of the world blew into his gaping nostrils and flung his hair writhing in all directions. Kei looked about him, and this is what he saw.

Looking down, he saw the reed thatching spread out in a great circle below him like the radiating spokes of a giant wheel. This circular roof was coloured rich brown and yellow and green with little grasses and growing flowers. And this was how the Wheel of the World was first known, from what Kei saw sticking his head up through the roof of King Arthur's house.

Looking east, Kei saw a red sphere rising over a distant flat line at the very rim of reality; this was tomorrow's sunrise, so far could he see from that roof that he saw it coming before today's sun had set. And Kei muttered into his beard, saying 'seeing tomorrow's sun doesn't find my flea . . .' and this was the first prophecy uttered in the land of Britain though not the last.

Next Kei looked west; he saw a great roaring purple sea with deep green waves crested by white frothing creamy foam; he saw fish leaping and spouting and sporting, and many islands floating to and fro yet never crashing into one another. He saw pluming fountains of water rising into the cloudfilled skies and circling back to fall as rain through vast wheeling flocks of birds that called and cried in many different tones and voices. In the depths he saw glimpses of a beast so large that even he had difficulty measuring its size. 'The world is wider than the land of Britain', Kei muttered into his salt-encrusted beard; and this was the first definition of geography ever made in Arthur's realm. Shaking the blown sea-weed and a goggling haddock from his hair, Kei turned to look south.

Southwards were the vast territories of the corrupt Empire of Rome, peopled by hot sweating midgets toiling under whip and lash to build houses tall enough for the incoming civilised soldiery who would soon take that Empire for their own, again and again and again. In the southern sky the great Invincible Sun roared and spread his wings in joy; he breathed out and blasted his worshippers with insufferable light and heat. Kei shook the drops of sweat from his forehead and gasped 'Rain is the healthiest of weather', and thus were the sciences of medicine, meteorology, psychology, and political economy created.

Kei made progress around the circle of the roof by turning and observing the spokes of radiating reed thatch that stretched out from the collar around his neck, which had once been a smoke-hole, to the very edge of the roof itself. Below this edge nothing could be seen, but he knew that the land of Britain lay somewhere beneath it; he counted the numbers of spokes as he turned east, west, and south, and thus by calculation he knew when he was facing north. So were mathematics and geometry defined for the first time.

As Kei looked north, he could hear faint sounds floating up from within the hall below the encircling roof; it was the company of Arthur, led by the King himself, clashing their golden wine cups together and singing, 'A flea, a flea . . .'. But these jovial noises were lost when Kei looked into the mirror of Night, where the stars live and move to ecstatic music in their spiral dance. So deep was the north that Kei opened both his eyes wide; he saw the shapes of Bear and Spindle, Dog and Weaver, but largest of all was the image of a Giant brandishing a club made from the shin-bone of an ox.

'Aha,' roared Kei, 'so it is you that stole my little flea!'

But the Star Hunter merely tightened up his belt, and took a step across eternity.

'Oho,' roared Kei, 'so it is Orion who stole Arthur's supper . . . I will have some satisfaction from you for this!'

But the Giant's shoulders soon filled the northern sky; storms sprang up across the Irish Sea, and the Atlantic heaved and tumbled until the song of 'Little flea' all up and down the length of Britain was utterly drowned out by the howling wind and lashing rain of winter.

Kei, barely able to breathe in the first onslaught of this terrible star Giant, finally looked upwards. His eyes narrowed as his vision sped towards the central pivot of all worlds; the roof-wheel fell away below him and the land of Britain seemed to shrink and tumble until it was a green speck in the purple ocean. Up he rose above the ever-breathing clouds and up until the world itself seemed little more than a smear of blue upon star-mirror . . .

But what Kei saw next is for another day, and in another story. Three things, then, to remember: never trust a short barbarian, never fall into the porridge, and never eat all of an ox or tell all of a tall tale at one sitting.

The Beheading Game

THE MAIN TALE in this sequence is primitive; it is found in Irish in its most direct variants, and as the remarkable legend of Gawain and the Green Knight in medieval developments. The features most important to Arthurian lore are those of honour, courage and typically a magical battle between life and death or summer and winter. This ancient battle occupied the imagination of Arthur's culture; if we could eavesdrop upon a sixth-century story-telling, we would undoubtedly hear a version of 'The Beheading Game'.

To give us some insight into the history of the period immediately preceding Arthur, and the role of bards and intelligencers in the complex political and military changes of the time, the tale is told by a British ambassador to the Emperor of the West. That there were networks of spies and informers, both Imperial and otherwise, is certain. The fact that our story-teller is given the title of 'Myrddin', which later became Merlin, is speculation based upon evidence. In other words, there was more than one Merlin, for the name was actually a title or description given to a particular type of druid, seer or bard.

Towards the close of the story, the teller utters a curious prophecy about Bears and Boars, and speculates upon how tradition will tell of the descendants of Ambrosius, the war duke. We know, of course, that Arthur followed shortly after the period in which this sequence is set, and that, as late as the twelfth century, prophecies about bears, boars, giants, dragons and other marvels were associated with Merlin and the history of Britain. It seems likely, though unproven, that the mysterious verses set out in Latin by Geoffrey of Monmouth are derived from a genuine Welsh or Breton sequence in an oral tradition stemming from at least as early as the fifth century. Thus a little poetic or perhaps prophetic licence has put bears and boars into the mouth of the bardic spy who entertains the Last Emperor of the West.

The Emperor of the West sat in his palace at Ravenna and thought long gloomy Imperial thoughts. He had much to trouble him; his head ached, his stomach burned, and the tramp of marching Germans training in the surrounding courtyards did not help at all. But mainly it was this other Emperor in the East who upset him, who had a better claim, who had not been set up by a German general. Yet Emperor of the West he was, even though he woke at nights sweating and feeling like a man of straw. Perhaps he was after all a false Emperor, and the other one in the east was true. How simple it had all been in the earlier days when there was only one Emperor, and he only had little things to concern himself with: poison, daggers of assassination, exotic diseases brought on by debauchery, madness, and the revenge of pagan gods and goddesses. The Emperor of the West did not have such clear-cut problems; he had Germans (well he was mainly German himself), bishops, invading savages who were really cousins, territorial claims, and many other complex matters. He gazed gloomily at the inlaid floor of his private chamber, brooding on the vast wealth of distant lands that was rightfully his but would never be realised.

The Empire was no longer centred on Rome . . . it was not centred anywhere.

In the corner his Greek physician stood ready with a compress of euphoric herbs; a masseur sat behind a discreet curtain, guarded by a stout Germanic warrior in fancy gilded uniform (masseurs were all suspect); three delightful young females sat at the opposite end of the chamber under the stern eye of their matron and procuress who had nodded greetings to the departing bishop as her scented party entered. From the passage to the kitchens, a silent procession of servants carried in sugared cakes, honeyed meats, sweet wine, spiced fish livers, whole tiny pigs' heads. All of these delicacies were rejected by a flick of the eyebrows from the Emperor's house-master, who was solely responsible for domestic matters in the private chamber. He considered none of these items new, thrilling, colourful or demanding enough for his master's present mood.

In short, the Emperor of the West was quite alone and very private at this time; he felt the fear of solitary rule (while wishing that he was the solitary and only Emperor) and dreaded a lonely death by boredom. The boots tramped on, the spears clashed, a constant reminder of where the power lay in Ravenna.

At length the Emperor lifted his little finger, left hand, very slightly. Immediately his favourite guard captain lumbered up to him and grunted. This communicative sound proved how concerned the chamber attendants were for their Emperor; normally the guards refused to speak to him at all unless directly ordered to do so.

'Bring me that story-teller from the land of Britain,' said the Emperor to the air in front of him, refusing to look at the soldier, 'the one that your men call Walu something or other. Make sure that he knows that I'm bored and in need of inspiration. I want to hear about battles . . . no, a combat

69

. . . something where the best one wins, the one who is really himself and not someone pretending to be something that he is not or should not be. There has to be a glorious struggle in which the best man wins, and people sing about it for years to come or write scrolls, and no churchmen to criticise. He must have something like that tucked away in his head; if he does not, beat one out of him.'

The guard grunted again and stamped off across the chamber, causing the girls to pretend to flinch, and scraping the delicate tiles with his nailed boots. His long blond hair had been carefully powdered and brushed for this duty, and floated over his gilded leather cuirass. He hoped that the Walu shaman was in a jovial mood, as no one would dare to lift a finger against such a magician, no matter what the silly little Emperor said. Life was so complex; he really had preferred living on a mound and clubbing his neighbours for pleasure; once a man acquired power and possessions such as boots, he was on the road to effete degradation. But the wine was good, and there was plenty of opportunity to develop skill in arms that could be turned against anyone . . . even a puppet Emperor.

As soon as the guard had left the chamber, the Emperor of the West felt unhappy concerning his request. This Walu Mertanus or whatever his ridiculous name was had come from Britain, of all places, two months ago. His presence had aroused considerable dispute among the Christian priests, though he too claimed to be Christian. What was worse, he claimed to represent one Ambrosius, a *dux bellorum* who was supposedly setting the abandoned province in order. The Emperor of the West had immediate visions of a rival . . . perhaps he would soon be known as the Emperor of the Middle, or the Emperor Between, or even the Previous Emperor. But far from uttering grandiose claims to power, this curious ambassador respectfully requested trading terms and a treaty of assistance and support; the Britons wanted heavy armour, modern weapons, larger horses. In return they would ship corn, wine and of course the old traditional commodity of hunting dogs, plus promised gifts of gold. None of this seemed remotely likely to the Emperor, who was not altogether stupid, and he kept the ambassador waiting in order to amuse himself. Perhaps if he waited long enough the *dux bellorum* might collapse under the weight of his pretentious title.

More immediate was the embarrassing fact that the Briton spoke immaculate antique Latin, in a high musical voice, with no uncouth German inflexions or bastard words. There was no question of him ever grunting '*Ych hyght Mertinus, Imperator*' or some such gibberish; he even used courtly phrases normally found only in Latin literature. He seemed more patrician than an old family from Rome itself, and this made the Emperor of the West feel slightly inferior.

So the Emperor had resorted to one of the most ancient ploys known to monarchs; he commanded Walu Mertinus to tell him stories; was the ambassador from Britain not after all a *bard*? The Emperor had innumerable spies, though he was uncertain who else they worked for; they advised him that the Briton had been growing restless and might be ready to depart, with or without Imperial permission. Only that evening a bishop had been blustering about heresy and pollution in connection with the Walu, and had demanded that he be banished. All the more reason, therefore, to keep him on a little longer. Let them all suffer even as their Emperor suffered, and the tale for tonight had better be a good one, or by the phantom of Julius Caesar someone would suffer even more! As soon as he had made this inward oath, the Emperor looked around him suspiciously . . . the great Julius had been cruelly murdered, and perhaps his phantom did not enjoy being invoked trivially by someone who, after all, represented everything that Julius had sought to keep out of the realms of Rome.

As the Emperor rested his head upon his fist to brood, there was heard a discreet, barely audible, coughing sound from a corner of the chamber. Looking up, he saw his favourite guard looming over him, and felt again that sudden terror of assassination; but having caught the Emperor's attention, the guard merely stepped aside to reveal the Walu. Being alone, thought the Emperor, has the advantage of no trumpets or proclamations or pedigrees, but it also means that people can sneak up and take you by surprise. Once again he looked with discomfort upon the British ambassador.

The Walu was tall; he wore a simple white woollen robe of the type sported by philosophers, astrologers, and similar mountebanks. With a graceful movement, he glided towards the Imperial dais. His hair was swept back and tied in a long horse-tail with silver wire; his beard had been neatly cut and trimmed. The long nose and firm mouth of the Walu seemed stern and critical, and the Emperor of the West barely managed to restrain himself from the urge to feel his own beard and moustaches. After the most minimal of prostrations, which caused many raised eyebrows and fluttering hands to mouths around the private chamber, the British bard stood waiting for the Emperor to speak, as was the custom.

'As my men will have informed you, I shall give further attention to your requests if you are able to entertain me. I require tonight a story that I have never heard before; it must have honour, terror, falsehood and the discovery of falsehood, a hero who wins against tremendous odds, and a general theme that persons must not imitate that which they are not, even if they truly think that they are whatever it may be . . . do you understand?' These last words were uttered slowly in the time-honoured manner of an emperor to a barbarian.

'Your request is immaculately phrased, great Imperial Warrior,' murmured the Walu in his perfect singsong Latin. He paused and closed his eyes for a moment, then continued: 'I have at my command the learned works of many authors; Homer, Horace, Virgilius, Socrates, Hecataeus, Solinus, or perhaps one of the modern poets . . . several of these have recounted tales similar to that which you seek.'

The Emperor of the West had not heard of some of the names mentioned, and loathed modern poets. He knew that the Briton was demonstrating his legendary bardic powers of memory to impress not only the ruler of the Empire (in the West) but everyone else who was with him while he sat alone in his private chamber. He tried to look bored, while thinking furiously of some source of tales that would flummox this self-satisfied savage from a forgotten colony. Suddenly, an extremely cunning thought came to him:

'No, nothing Greek, or Roman, or modern; nothing political, or geographical or doctrinal; I've heard it all before and find it dull. Do you not have a repertoire from . . .' and here he paused, ready to devastate Walu Mertinus with a request that even a bard would find hard to accommodate, 'your native land?' There, he had said it. Everyone knew that Britain, though rich in corn and farmland, had no writing or literature of its own; everything had been borrowed from the civilisation and influence of Rome. There was no evidence that they had any literature whatsoever, other than heretical religious nonsense that occasionally found its way across the sea to Gaul.

Mertinus drew himself upright; first he frowned, then he smiled. This is a good sign, thought the Emperor; he's worried but he's faking pleasure.

'Yes, Imperator, most assuredly we do have a small

collection of miserable tales in my native country. But they are hardly suitable for such discerning and august ears as your own.'

Just as I thought, the Emperor smiled almost openly. 'Poor though they may be, I expect that they will have a certain remote and bucolic charm. Perhaps you can find one suitable to my needs . . . do you require time? I can allow you the turning of a sand-glass to prepare any scrolls or clerical assistants who can read and prompt.'

'Oh indeed not, most refulgent and opulent ruler,' came the instant reply. 'If your Imperial person will permit I am able to proceed directly from memory.'

'Ah, yes. Well . . . proceed . . . do you require a stool? No? Good, carry on as directed.' And the Emperor flicked the third finger of his left hand, upon which sign the guard captain hurried out to stop the drilling and crunching and grinding and shouting from outside. The march of boots turned into scurrying and scampering, and a few lewd shouts floated over the night wind. Then there was silence, and the bard began to speak softly in his perfect rhythmic Latin. As he spoke the guards made signs to ward off spirits, but they crowded round the chamber door to listen.

'Let all who have ears listen, and may the tale be remembered forever. This is the tale of the Beheading Game and the Warrior from the land of Summer, told this day by Myrddin of the Cymri in the Imperial hall at Ravenna.

'Once long ago in the land of Britain there was a great king who held his warriors to a yearly pact; every year they must come to the royal hall for feasting, games, combat, and a competition to establish the king's champion for the year to come. And the king was called Bran in the British tongue, which is of course Brennus in Latin, and simply means 'leader'.

'As evening drew on, the company were seated in the hall

74

eating and drinking and boasting. The doors flew open with a loud blast of howling wind and the door pins shattered and flew across the room to impale a Greek physician who stood mixing remedies for the wounded champions after the games. With a trembling of the floor from the great weight of his bear-skin clad feet, a horrible ugly giant of a man strode in and glared all around. He was wrapped in a mottled bull-hide and carried a living green tree in one broad hand, with its roots in the dark earth and its crown reaching up almost to the roofbeams of the hall. In his other hand, with fingers as broad as a warrior's wrist, he held an axe with a bronze head greater than the doors of the temple of Minerva in Rome itself. The handle would have taken a team of six great ploughing oxen to move it, but the sharpness of the blade-edge was so keen that a mere hair blown against it in a gentle breeze would be instantly split into two parts.

'This towering warrior burst through the assembled ranks, and trampled upon a masseur who had tried to hide under a bench. He took his stance right beside the great roof-support in the centre of the hall, where the undying fire burned winter and summer through.

'The king's house-master and steward spoke up saying: "Why do you burst in here and stand by the roof pole, blocking the fire? Do you wish to be burnt to death? I fear that the heat of your anger will destroy this hall rather than benefit it!"

' "Well spoken, little man," rumbled the warrior, shaking his green tree over the cowering heroes, "Whatever my powers are, you will all soon agree that I come to enlighten rather than to incinerate; no matter how much I glow, the hall of this king will never be destroyed. But light is not my only power, I have others also, but even the powers that I have cannot satisfy my quest."

75

'At this the king spoke up: "If you come as supplicant, I bid you tell of the nature of your quest, for this is the annual gathering of champions, where all great deeds may be performed with honour."

'At this kingly statement the green-branched warrior smiled and radiated heat . . . "I have been in Erin, in Alba, in Gaul and in Europe; in Africa and Asia and Greece and Scythia; in the Islands of Gades, the Pillars of Hercules, in the Tower of Bregon and the mountains of India; I have been in Summer Lands, and over Earth, and under Sea; my intelligence has reached to the furthest lights set by the Creator in the vault of Heaven, but never have I found a man who understands fair play." At this the company roared and protested and shouted and blustered that they were heroes all, and any one of them could show fair play, even to a giant who shed light as easily as a procuress sheds fleas.

' "Very well," rumbled the warrior, and his breath blew away a procession of cooks who brought meat to the royal table. "As you men of Britain excel all others in strength, prowess, valour, nobility, generosity, excellence, wit, dignity, honesty, truth and worth, you shall select a champion from among yourselves to satisfy my quest. But because of the sacred nature of his kingship, Bran shall be spared this test, for he shall act as a bridge across stormy waters in the times to come. Let a hero stand forth to prove he understands fair play."

'The warriors were silent, fearing some kind of trick. Finally, a great fat-necked, muscular, thick-skulled warrior asked as to the nature of the proof.

' "Easy is the answer to that question, little man, for I seek merely a bargain of fair play in which I cut off your head tonight and you in turn cut off mine tomorrow night." The fat-necked warrior, renowned for his strength at wrestling and his ability to think no thoughts for long periods of time, turned pale and said: 'I'll take the challenge on the condition that you turn it the other way around, and let me have first blow."

' "So the men of Britain are as flatulent and soggy as the rest of the world," roared the giant, shaking his tree and blasting the company with the heat of his face. "Nevertheless I will turn the bargain around and agree to take the first blow." And he immediately lay down with his head on the chopping block, and pushed his axe into the hands of the fat-necked warrior. The blow was struck with great enthusiasm, straight through the giant's neck and on into the block did the huge sharp axe fall. The fountain of blood sluiced across the floor of the hall and flushed away two bishops who had but recently come into the land to preach.

'For an instant the giant corpse lay still, then, clutching his green tree as if it were a staff, the headless body slowly drew himself upright. He snatched at his fallen head, and stuck it back upon his shoulders, and taking tree, axe, chopping block and all, hurled himself from the hall of the king, straight out through the stout wall, which ripped apart like cloth.'

Suddenly Walu Mertinus paused, and seemed to mop his brow as if he too had felt the heat of the green warrior. The Emperor of the West sat rigid upon his throne; the symbolism of the tale had not been lost on him, and he saw it as an allegory of his futile wars against the invading tribes from the north and north-east. He also knew that there was some other subtle meaning to the tale just beyond his reach.

The German guards grinned at one another; they had liked the scene where the bishops were flushed away by blood . . . as for the rest it was a typical magician's story and was certain to have a tricky ending. The shaman was not chanting, however, and seemed suddenly to look around the room as if he had lost something. Just as the Emperor was

77

about to lift a finger, Mertinus gave a visible start and rushed back into the telling.

'Yes . . . when the mysterious giant warrior returned the following evening, the fat-necked one had run away and broken his covenant. But with furious words and taunts he made another stout veteran strike off his head; once again he recovered from the blow, and once again the covenant was broken by a Briton who dared not receive his blow in fair play. On the third night of this contest, the king's personal champion returned from hunting, bearing a fine stag with ten points. The quality of this man was that he could grow short and broad or long and thin at will, and with his skill at arms and his speed in hunting, he had never lost a battle.

'The hero took one look at the green warrior stretched out upon the blood-stained block, and leaping forward snatched up the great axe. High he lifted it until it touched the roof of the hall; hard he hefted it until it clove through the air, neck, bone, block and floor. To this very day there is a cleft in the ground in that place where the River Avon flows into the Severn sea, and a sacred cavern dedicated to the giant may still be seen by those brave enough to climb up to it.

'But even this blow did not prevent the glowing warrior from picking up his head, clapping it onto his blood-clotted shoulders, and stamping off into the night. "I shall be back tomorrow, little man," he bellowed, "and I will have sharpened my axe!"

'All the next day the king's personal champion sat in dread, and a few unkind members of the court started singing funeral songs. When night fell there was no feasting in that hall, and the fire burned dim. Just at midnight the doors crashed open and the fearsome warrior made his presence felt with a blast of heat and the smell of green leaves and growing plants bursting from the earth.

' "Stretch out your neck, little man," he bellowed, flinging down the chopping block.

'The champion slowly stepped up to the block and laid his head upon it; a gasp went round the assembly.

' "Not long enough, little short neck . . . stretch further still." And the champion stretched his spine so that a warrior's full grown foot would have fitted between any two of his ribs, and his skin was pale with the stretching and his face red. But now his neck lay full across the death block, and the giant raised his axe . . .'

Now in the very midst of this drama, the Emperor of the West biting his knuckles and the guards climbing over one another to peep through the curtain, Walu Mertinus coughed again, and uttered a muffled word or two breaking up the metre of the verse as if he had lost the next line altogether.

Immediately a servant leapt forward with chilled wine and sugared fruits, but the bard waved these refreshments away. The Emperor could hardly contain himself from asking what would happen next . . . but it would be too much to show curiosity to this pedlar from over the western sea . . . this supplicant for aid in the midst of chaos and ruin. The Emperor signed the servant to his dais, and took wine to mask his eagerness for the tale to continue. As he drank, he studied the bard over the rim of his goblet. Was his face flushed red again? Surely he was blushing; had he actually *forgotten* how to begin the next verse? But his powers of memory were supernatural . . . or so he had posed and postured earlier in the evening.

With a deliberate show of imperial impatience, the Emperor allowed his fingers to drum lightly upon the arms of his throne. The servants turned pale, the house-master lifted his eyebrows several inches and began to sidle towards the chamber door. Behind the curtain, the German guards looked at each other in slow puzzlement; they knew that these western shamans had magical powers of memory and could not understand this embarrassing incident which would surely lose Walu Mertinus much prestige.

Once more the Walu cleared his throat and looked about him; the Emperor could resist no longer.

'So your powers of recollection are not as great as you would have us think, man of Britain. Perhaps it is the change of climate or the intimacy of the situation. It seems that you lose your wager with us; for if you cannot keep a simple boast, how can you keep a bargain concerning arms and materials? How do we know that your *dux bellorum* will not forget how much he has to pay?' The Walu grew dark red in the face and gasped for breath, as if indignant and outraged. But the Emperor was on sure ground now ... 'Enough play-acting, Mertinus Walu, we will revise our bargain. If you can complete the tale as agreed, you will live. If not you will have your head cut off at one blow by the captain of my guard ... and no power in the world will bring *you* back to strike a return blow!'

Behind the curtain the guards pushed and elbowed to be out from under the touch of their captain, who up to now had leant in a comradely fashion upon their shoulders. If he had to kill the shaman he would be the most unlucky man in Ravenna, perhaps in the whole world. Just as it seemed likely that the captain's luck had finally turned for the worse, the shaman cleared his throat again, and fumbled his way through a few lines from the previous verse of the tale. Suddenly he launched into the final scene with great power and a fine sense of rhythm. The German guards sighed and settled down to listen.

'The sound of the axe rising and the giant's bull-hide coat creaking were as loud as the tempests that toss the forest of Calydon on a winter night. There was a sound such as is made by a hundred eagles plunging for the kill with air whistling through their pinions, and the invincible axe came down upon the champion's neck; halting short, blunt side first.

' "Rise up, little man," roared the green warrior, his face glowing with pleasure. "You are incomparable for valour, for courage, and for fair play; henceforth let all the men of Britain look to you for an example, and if your totem is the boar, as I see it is from your round shield, then a bear will bear the boar as an example to the world."

'And with these enigmatic words, the mysterious warrior vanished.'

At dawn the Emperor drank a draught of watered wine mixed with a mild purgative, and wondered what the Emperor of the East had been prescribed by his physician. Secretaries and advisors gathered around armed with papers and petitions and information, while the churchmen muttered crossly to one another with much waving of arms and citing of references.

Just as he lifted a finger to commence the day's business, his favourite guard captain lumbered into the hall and whispered loudly in the Emperor's ear.

'The magician has vanished just like his giant.' The Emperor of the West was not good at riddles before noon, and stared blankly at his captain, trying to recollect if this was perhaps a code word for the day or for covert action against some group of dissidents.

'The Britisher, the Walu; he charmed himself over the guest-block walls into the night. He has taken three Imperial post horses!' For a short moment there was silence, then pandemonium broke loose as the Emperor of the West grew red then black in the face, stood up and gasped for breath. Slaves, doctors, advisors, clerics and burly warriors started

81

running hither and thither, smashing into one another, trampling upon bare toes with studded boots, knocking over maps and inks and scrolls and stylii. But rage as he might, the Emperor of the West never saw a bard again.

The bard who bore the honoured title of Myrddin relaxed for the first time in seven months. The journeys through the restless vicious lands had been tedious and dangerous, but now he was on a ship from Little Britain, heading westwards into the refreshing sea rain and mist. The angelic British tongue was spoken all around him, and he was given some genuine respect and privacy. Not that he was a proud man, but it had been hard indeed to be treated as a mere entertainer and clown. How degenerate the Empire had grown; perhaps Britain really was the last haven of the light, just as Ambrosius insisted during his fiery speeches.

Telling the head-severing tale to that ridiculous puppet Emperor had been hard; Myrddin knew that he had over-done the loss of memory, but these barbarians were used to overacting and were often unable to detect subtleties . . . so the crude and obvious had to be employed openly. The Greek had worried him; they were a cunning people and probably had British ancestry somewhere in them before they had declined, or so it seemed from their literature. But the physician had understood the open threat in the tale, as had the old witch of a procuress. And the masseur would have said nothing anyway, being already well paid for information. Pity that the crack about the bishops was wasted, though it served to amuse the guards for a while.

A bard's memory was indeed as Myrddin had claimed for himself: perfect. In addition to the great works of Greece and Rome, Egypt, Chaldea and the vast Eastern lands beyond the known world, the Christian gospel (in all sect-arian variants), modern historians and geographers and the vast oral repertoire of his own national poems, wisdom tales, initiatory dramas, alphabets, animal and bird lore, astronomy, cosmology, and extensive genealogy, Walu Mertinus now knew the strength of the Imperial armies in the West. He also knew the weaknesses of the officers, and what revolts were planned; what tribes were about to invade by land and by sea, and which of the savages had blood relatives in the Imperial court. He also knew a name-list of informers and the means to contact them, and a network of seamen and fisherfolk who would not hesitate to warn of a forthcoming fleet of barbarians . . . be they Imperial or otherwise.

He, Myrddin, would take this store back to the *dux bellorum*, who would use it not only to defend Britain, but to take as much of Europe as he could to declare a new Roman Empire. But the bard was uncertain about these greater ambitions; he knew that the strength of the Britons was also their weakness, the love of poetry and images over attention to facts and details. Ambrosius might be able to organise in the old Roman style, but it would not be likely to reach beyond the shores of the Island of the Mighty into neighbouring Gaul, other than through the present network of trade, friends and relatives, and of course spies. The British warriors lived as much in the land of the Fair Folk or the mysteries of Light as they did in the saddle or at the tower of a fighting ship. Even if Ambrosius did not sweep through Gaul into Germany and perhaps on even to Rome itself, the bards would eventually sing as if his dreams had become history. And then compose verses about some unborn son who would follow in his father's path.

As the salt spray washed across his face, Walu Mertinus, Myrddin by title in the ancient manner, pulled his high pointed hood down over his head, relaxed into the hard wooden bulwark of the vessel, and prepared to sleep in safety. What, he thought, was truth?

Owein of the Ravens

THE STORY OF Owein of the Ravens, or as it is more properly called *Rhonabwy's Dream*, comes from the premier source of ancient Welsh lore and legend collected under the title of *The Mabinogion*. It is here that we find perhaps the most significant descriptions of Arthur's warriors; not, as one might expect, couched in the language or fashion of the twelfth century, when it was first written down, but bearing all the hallmarks of the sixth-century warriors upon whom so many of Arthur's knights are based.

The intricate and detailed descriptions of clothing and weapons are unparalleled anywhere else, and are the reason why this story is said to be impossible to tell from memory, as the ancient bardic story-tellers once did with all their lore and history.

Owein himself appears in the medieval romances as Sir Uwain, the son of Arthur's greatest adversary King Urien of Gore. In fact, both Urien and Owein are historically attested figures, who had bardic laments written about them which are still extant. Urien was king of the Strathclyde area of northern Britain, either in the same period or shortly after that of Arthur. There is an extant early Welsh lament commemorating Owein's death in which he is described as 'reaper of foes' and 'a despoiler'.

Of the strange game played by Arthur and Owein in this story, much speculation has gone into its nature. It is clearly a board-game related to chess, though scholarly consensus is that it is *not* chess. Another speculation points to the Irish game of fidchel. Little more is known about this game than about gwyddbwyll, but it does offer one clue to the nature of the conflict between Arthur and Owein. In fidchel, as in chess, the king is the most important piece and is defended by a series of knights; however, significantly, the king's defenders are less in number than that of his adversaries, whose task it is to capture him. If we assume for the moment that gwyddbwyll was a similar kind of game and that Arthur was the King (in both senses of the word) and Owein's Ravens his opponents . . . then we may begin to see aspects of the story in a new light.

In our story, as in the original version, the battle between Arthur and his nephew is a symbolic or magical struggle carried on within the framework of a dream. We have chosen to suggest that the Ravens were an actual group of fighting men, although in the original this is ambiguous enough to give one pause. However, the raven was the symbol of the Celtic battle goddess, the Morrigan, and there are enough literary references to the bloody work of these battleground scavengers to suggest the underlying nature of the tale. Perhaps also, buried deeply within the old text, is a reference to the difficulties experienced by Arthur in trying to weld the proud, wild, passionate-natured Celtic tribesmen into a fighting unit alongside the Romano-British descendants of the Legions which had always been the tribesmen's enemy.

There was once a man called Iorweth ap Maredudd who desired greatly to be overlord of Powys instead of his brother Madawg – however, this story does not concern him at all and so we shall not hear of him again. It concerns rather one of his men who was called Rhonabwy, and a certain dream that he had while sleeping on the skin of a yellow ox in the house of Heilyn the Red, son of Cawgawn, son of Iddon, son of . . . well, never mind who he was the son of – let us hear about Rhonabwy's dream.

This was the way of it: Rhonabwy thought that he was riding towards the Ford of the Cross at Havren in the Kingdom of Powys and that he saw coming towards him a figure that gave him cause to feel fear. The figure was of a warrior dressed in green from the waist down, with a tunic of gold brocade sewn with green thread, and at his thigh a gold-hilted sword in a sheath of best cordovan leather. Over all he wore a mantle of yellow brocade with patterns upon it sewn with green silk, and he rode a spirited, high-stepping horse which covered the ground so swiftly that he overtook Rhonabwy in two breaths. Such was the size of the warrior that Rhonabwy, even when mounted upon his horse, reached only to his thigh.

And Rhonabwy gave him very polite greeting and asked to know who he was.

'Iddawg is my name, son of Mynyo. But I am better known by my nickname which is the Church of Britain.'

'Why are you called that?' asked Rhonabwy.

'Because I was one of the messengers between Arthur and Medrawt before the Battle of Camlan, and every good word that Arthur spoke I made to sound like an insult, for I was young and eager and I desired very greatly that there should be battle between the two of them.'

Now, even in his dream, Rhonabwy knew that the Battle of Camlan had taken place many hundreds of years before and that all these men had died there, including Arthur and Medrawt – though some still told a tale about Arthur being taken away by three Royal Women to a mysterious island somewhere in the West. Rhonabwy knew of course, as all sensible people know these days, that such things were merely fables designed to entertain men of simple minds – yet here he stood in the presence of a giant warrior who claimed he had been at Camlan, and this did not seem like a fable.

'Three days before the battle ended, I went to Scotland to do penance for my wicked deeds, but now I am returning to the Camp of Arthur to join in the hosting of the Ravens. If you wish, you shall ride with me. . . .'

This seemed to make even less sense to Rhonabwy, because if Arthur had been killed at Camlan along with all his warriors, then how was it possible for Iddawg to be going to *visit* him?

While he was thinking this, another warrior upon a great black horse rode towards them. He was clad in red brocade sewn with yellow silk, and his mantle was fringed with gold. He swiftly overtook Rhonabwy and Iddawg and asked who was this little fellow that Iddawg had found; and though he did not much like being called a 'little fellow', Rhonabwy had to admit the truth of it and so he kept silent while the two warriors conversed.

And Iddawg explained that he had found Rhonabwy upon the plain, and that he had invited him to ride to the hosting of the Ravens. And the two fell to talking of who would be present and Rhonabwy listened in astonishment to the names of the heroes who were believed long dead in his time but who, it seemed, were coming together to fight a great battle against Osla Big-Knife at a place called Caer Faddon. And he heard much of one Owein, nephew of Arthur, whose warriors were called 'Ravens' and from whom he might look for 'entertainment' when he arrived at the camp.

And so the two huge warriors, with Rhonabwy riding between them (struggling to keep up, if the truth be told) crossed the plain of Argyngrog and came to the ford of Rhyd y Groes on the Hafren; and there they found the tents of Arthur set up along the side of the road. And on a little flat islet in the centre of the river, the pavilion of Arthur was set up. And Arthur himself stood before it with a bishop upon his one side and a slender dark youth upon his other.

Rhonabwy stood in the presence of one already deemed fabulous and who, from his great size alone, could never be taken for a mortal. For Arthur was like a man of bronze, with his ruddy skin and red-gold hair, and beard streaming down upon his breast. So powerful was he indeed that it seemed to Rhonabwy that he almost emitted a glow of light.

Iddawg and his companion (who was called Rhufawn) got down from their horses and splashed across the river to greet their lord. Rhonabwy hung back until Arthur saw him and demanded to know whence he came. When Iddawg explained, Arthur looked down at Rhonabwy and was silent. At length he sighed and said: 'To think that men of his kind shall come to rule this land, after those who ruled it before them,' which confused Rhonabwy deeply since it seemed impossible to him that he should be in the presence of so great and ancient a figure who yet addressed him as a man of the future.

While this exchange had been taking place a great commotion began along the river, and looking in that direction, Rhonabwy saw a second host of men approaching. They were dressed in black from head to foot, except for the fringes upon their mantles, which were of pure white, and they each had a tuft of ravens' feathers upon their helmets or about their persons, and the banner they bore was a raven upon a white ground.

Arthur stood up then and called: 'Welcome, Owein, son of Urien – welcome to the Ravens.' And one rode forward into the water upon his high-stepping black horse and called back: 'Greetings to the War-Lord, Arthur; greetings, uncle.' And Rhonabwy looked with keen interest to see this famed figure whose death-song had been sung by no lesser bard than Taliesin Pen Beirdd. He saw a tall slender youth with shining black hair and eyes the colour of cornflowers, and a look of confidence about him that warned of a high-metalled spirit. And he saw that although many of the warriors of Arthur greeted the Ravens of Owein, yet the latter chose to make camp on the farther bank of the river. But he was distracted from thinking such thoughts by Iddawg, who called to him to come and watch the arming of Arthur. 'For', said he, 'the Host must be at Caer Faddon by midday to meet with Osla Big-Knife, and the Lord must first be armed for battle.'

Then Rhonabwy saw a small hairy man with a great scarlet face come forward, and he had in his arms the sword of Arthur, that was named Caledfwlch, having a design of two serpents upon the hilt. When the sword was drawn it was as though fire came from the mouths of these creatures in two flames, and the light was such that no one might look at it. Then from a great pack, the small man drew forth a scarlet mantle with an apple of red-gold at each corner, and placed it about the shoulders of the Lord, and Rhonabwy remembered that it was said of this mantle, which was called Gwenn, that when it was wrapped about the body of the man who wore it, none might see where he walked, though *he* might see all that he wished.

And so the arming went on, with Arthur's shield, Prydwen, with its magical likeness of the God's Mother painted upon it, and Arthur's knife, Carnwennan, that could cut the very air, and his mighty spear Rhongommiant, that no amount of living men could turn aside – until at last the warrior stood ready and the Great Dragon standard was unfurled at the head of its staff and the whole host stood ready to depart. And at that moment Owein came forward from the press of men gathered about their Lord, and said loudly: 'Uncle, will you play a game of gwyddbwyll with me?' and there was a sudden silence over all the throng.

Rhonabwy waited for Arthur to speak angrily to his nephew, but instead he merely smiled and said to the small man who carried his weapons, 'Eiryn, fetch me the board and the pieces.' And he called for two chairs and sat down and, when the gwyddbwyll board had been brought, Arthur and Owein began to play, while the rest of the host sat down to await the outcome of the game.

Now, when they were deeply into the game, a messenger hurried up to Arthur and said: 'Lord, the Ravens are attacking your men and are killing them with beak and claw!' And Arthur paused in his play and said: 'Nephew, call off your Ravens!' But Owein merely looked at the gwyddbwyll board and said, 'Your move, Lord.'

And so they continued to play, and all the time Rhonabwy, who did not quite dare to go and look, could hear the sound of a great commotion coming from the far side of the river.

Presently, when Arthur and Owein had finished one game of gwyddbwyll, and had begun another, a second messenger rode up in a lather of sweat and cried out to Owein that Arthur's warriors had turned upon the Ravens and were inflicting terrible slaughter upon them; then it was Owein's turn to ask that Arthur call off his men. But Arthur merely said: 'Play on, nephew.' And so they played, until a third warrior rode up and he was dressed all in green and gold, with a helmet with a dragon's crest the eyes of which blazed so furiously that no one dared look at them. And this messenger cried out that there was terrible slaughter between Arthur's warriors and Owein's Ravens, and that soon

91

there would be a scarcely a whole man among either host. Then Arthur stood up and took four of the pieces in each of his great hands and crushed them to golden powder, and Owein looked at that work and, calling forward one of his retinue, told him to lower the standard of the Ravens. And at that there was peace between both sides and Arthur and Owein shook hands.

Rhonabwy, who had watched all this in some astonishment, shook his head over the strange actions of heroes (mythical or not) and turned to look for Iddawg for clarification. But the giant warrior only smiled and shrugged, and pointed to a ring that sparkled upon Arthur's finger. 'See that,' he said, 'that is the ring of Arthur, and it has the property that will enable you to remember all that you have seen tonight.'

At that moment a warrior came up to Arthur and said that Osla Big-Knife had asked for a truce until a fortnight hence and what should be his answer? And Arthur said that he would grant the truce, so that both he and Owein might have time to reassemble the fragments of the host and be ready for the battle. And he got upon his great war steed from which he towered above all men there, and in a great voice said, 'Let all those who would take part in this battle with me meet upon the field of Caer Faddon in a fortnight in the morning. And those who shall not, need not.' And he gave a great laugh and looked (Rhonabwy thought) straight at him. Then the camp began to break up, and in the noise and bustle of that Rhonabwy awoke; and whether he was a wiser man for the dream that he dreamt upon the yellow ox-skin, or whether he was not, I cannot say, but I believe that he went away and spoke long and deeply to the two brothers who wished to be kings of Powys. Though whether they listened to him or not, I know not, for this is the end of the tale of Rhonabwy's dream and nothing else need concern us.